THE ORPHAN'S SCANDAL

VICTORIAN SAGA ROMANCE

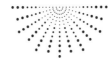

JESSICA WEIR

SWEETBOOKHUB.COM

WELCOME TO MY VICTORIAN WORLD

I am delighted that you are reading one of my Victorian Romances. It is a pleasure to share it with you. I hope you will enjoy reading them as much as I enjoyed writing them.

I would like to invite you to join my exclusive Newsletter. You will be the first to find out when my books are available. Join now, it is completely FREE, and I will send you The Foundling's Despair FREE as a thank you.

~

You can find all my books on Amazon, click the yellow follow button, and Amazon will let you know when I have new releases and special offers.

Much love,

Jessica

CHAPTER ONE

"You're in a world of your own, Florence," Marcus Daventry said, sneaking up on her and seemingly delighted that he almost scared her clean out of her skin.

"Marcus!" Florence said in a harsh tone as she stooped to pick up the wooden clothes peg she had dropped on the flagstones of the back yard. "What are you doing here? If my Grandma catches you, she'll have your guts for garters!"

"Why? What did I do this time?" Marcus's bright blue eyes danced with amusement.

"You ate the raisin biscuits she made." Florence, who

was getting over the shock, began to see the funny side.

"Not all of them," Marcus said in a plaintiff tone as he shrugged.

"You left two behind! In Queenie's book, you ate the lot, or as near to it as makes no difference."

"She really is going to have my guts for garters, isn't she?" His rueful look made Florence laugh.

Marcus Daventry had a wonderful relationship with Florence's grandmother. Even though Queenie Smith was the house servant, Marcus always treated her with respect, even when he was teasing her. Florence knew her grandmother adored him, having seen him grow from a boy of just four into a young man of seventeen.

"I don't know why you antagonise her the way you do, Marcus. You know you will be the worse for it in the end. And this time, I reckon she'll take the broom to you!"

"You're not making me feel any better."

"I'm not trying to." Florence laughed, as she pegged her last sheet to the line in the little drying yard.

"Won't you offer a condemned man some final comfort?" he went on, grinning.

"Condemned men don't smile like that. You're being dramatic."

"Only thirteen years old, and you are so much cleverer than I am, Florence. You see through me with those shrewd blue eyes of yours. Perhaps they are too blue for your own good."

"But your eyes are blue. Even bluer than mine, I think."

"I hadn't realised you'd ever looked," he teased, and the two of them looked into their respective blue eyes for a moment.

It was a moment that made Florence feel a little breathless. Surely, she'd looked into his eyes over the thirteen years she had lived in his parents' fine Wimbledon home and not felt as peculiar as she did at that moment. Surely, she had never felt that strange swirl of energy in her stomach and the heat which began at her throat and worked its way upward until her cheeks changed colour.

Something was changing, and Florence had the

strongest sense that it was her. She was thirteen now, and she was somehow seeing Marcus Daventry differently these days. He'd looked this way for a long time; a little more manly than he had once done. His hair was as dark as hers was fair, and those blue eyes of his, almost the same colour as her own, stood out like gemstones, always twinkling with merriment and light.

Marcus was tall, a good foot taller than her, and he was filling out. She could hardly remember the point at which his youthful slightness had been replaced with a lean broadness which spoke of strength and manhood. Next to him, she felt like a child, and she wondered how long it would be before he tired of her company. Soon, he would no longer be interested in the little girl who had been his friend, it was inevitable as their lives went in different directions.

Florence bit her lip to put an end to the thought. She couldn't bear the idea of Marcus having his head turned by an older girl, a pretty girl of his own class, as he surely must sooner or later. No, it would do Florence Smith no good to indulge the burgeoning feelings of romance only to have them dashed by the reality of a system of class which had been in place in England for hundreds and hundreds of years. As nice and as kind as Mr and Mrs Daventry had been, and despite the fact that they had known Florence her entire life, she knew that they couldn't possibly consent to such a thing as a union between their only son and the motherless granddaughter of one of their servants. It just wasn't done.

"You're miles away again, only this time you don't even have the line of washing to blame it on. What are you thinking about?" Marcus asked, teasing her by tugging at the empty linen basket that she'd picked up ready to take back indoors. "Well? What are you thinking about?"

"I'm thinking that if you keep pulling at the linen basket, I'll just let go of it suddenly and you'll fall on your behind on the flagstones." Florence laughed, trying to hide behind amusement when she knew she could never tell him what she had been thinking.

"You wouldn't, you're not cruel enough," Marcus laughed and continued to tug at the basket. He was so much bigger and stronger than Florence that he easily pulled her along.

"Aren't I?" Florence said and grinned at him before suddenly letting go of the basket. As predicted,

Marcus, who was still tugging at the thing with some force, toppled backwards and landed square on his behind on the flagstones.

"You win!" he said, laughing as he sat on the ground with the empty linen basket in his lap.

"You'd better get up," Florence said, laughing but feeling a little sense of panic too. "If your mother looks out of one of the windows and sees you messing about here with me, sitting on the ground, she won't be very pleased."

"I hardly think she'd noticed these days," Marcus said, getting to his feet and brushing down the seat of his trousers.

"Why ever not?" Florence asked, seeing the look of uncertainty in those blue eyes. It was a look she had seen before in the last weeks, a look which had worried her from time to time.

Marcus Daventry was light and merriment; he never looked uncertain or distracted, and she had the greatest sense that it was a cause for concern.

"I don't know, not really," he began, setting the basket down on the flagstones and thrusting his hands into the pockets of the smart dark tweed trousers which matched his waistcoat perfectly. "I just know something is going on."

"What do you mean something is going on?"

"Something is going on between my mother and father," he went on. All the mischief was gone from his handsome face, to be replaced by a look which was somewhere between worried and a little embarrassed. Perhaps he was embarrassed to be admitting his own misgivings to her.

"You know whatever you tell me will stay with me, don't you? You know me well enough to know that," Florence said, truly meaning it and knowing that if he didn't tell her now, she would feel terribly hurt. She had set them both up and she knew it. However, it seemed that he was in a mood to get things off his chest.

"I know, Florence." He nodded his head, confirming his trust in her, making her feelings for him grow more and more. "The problem is, I don't really know what it is myself. There's an atmosphere between them... as if they're both worried about something. Maybe even afraid," he said, and he looked so concerned now that Florence felt a little afraid herself.

"Have you tried asking them what the matter is?"

"No," he said and shook his head slowly from side to side. "I know they won't tell me. Every time I walk into the drawing room, they look up sharply, stop talking, and everything feels very awkward. It has never been like that before, and so I suppose it makes me feel worse and worse. It makes me realise that something really is very wrong."

"I wish there was something I could do to help," Florence said sincerely.

"I know. I know you would help if you could, but I can't even help myself at the moment. Without knowledge, what can one do?"

They stood for some moments just looking at one another before Marcus took a single step towards her. The fingers of her right hand seemed to dance this way and that, and she knew that she wanted to reach out to him, to take his hand or to lay hers on his arm, something that would comfort him. This was new territory, a place that neither one of them had been before, and Florence was ashamed to admit that she was terrified of making a fool of herself. She was terrified of getting it wrong, even if there was a chance that she could have comforted him.

"Oh, there you are!" The unmistakable Cockney tone of her grandmother, Queenie Smith, freed them both from the strange little spell which held them as tightly as if they had been chained together. "And just what do you expect me to do with just two little raisin biscuits, young man?"

"When you think about it, Queenie, it's a compliment," Marcus said, and it was as if a hypnotist had clicked his fingers and returned him to his old self. His eyes were bright, his ready, handsome smile fully apparent.

"How so?" Queenie was marching across the yard with her hands on her hips.

"You are such an incredible baker, my dear, that even a man of reasonable firmness such as myself couldn't resist such delightful raisin biscuits." Marcus was grinning at the old woman, and Florence just knew that her grandmother was itching to laugh.

"Reasonable firmness? You don't have a shred of willpower when it comes to sweet treats, my boy!"

Queenie went on, scolding him in that warm and wonderful way she had done since he was a little boy. He was almost a man now, but it seemed that Queenie *hadn't* noticed in the same way that Florence had.

"All right, I surrender," Marcus said and held his hands out in front of him, his wrist together as if he expected Florence's grandmother to D cuffs on him and lead him away. "I'm ready to accept my punishment."

"Good, then you can run down to Arlo's grocery and bring back the sack of flour he has waiting for me, then I will be able to make some more biscuits!" There was a glint in Queenie's pale grey eyes which suggested that the great biscuit theft of old London town was about to work in her favour. She would much rather make a few more biscuits that afternoon than walk down to the grocer to collect the flour herself. Flour which she undoubtedly needed for more than just a few biscuits.

"I shall go this minute, my dear Queenie," Marcus said and performed an amusing, elaborate bow before turning to quickly wink at Florence. As he walked away, Queenie clicked her tongue and Florence hope she wasn't blushing.

"**F**lorence, are you helping or hindering, child?" Queenie asked with an air of gentle exasperation.

The two were folding large bedsheets, and Queenie stood impatiently waiting for Florence to walk towards her holding the two opposite corners.

"Sorry, Grandma," Florence said and laughed, hastening across the kitchen floor and handing the corners to Queenie before stooping to pick up the newly folded corners.

"You're daydreaming, Florence. What's the matter?"

"Nothing is the matter, Grandma."

"Yes, there is!" Queenie said, snatching the new corners from Florence and folding the last part herself. "Do you forget I raised you? I surely know when my very own granddaughter is troubled by something. Now then, out with it!"

"All right, you win, but it's nothing very important." Florence knew that wasn't entirely true. She had the greatest sense that it was something very, very important indeed, even if she didn't know quite what it was.

"Well?" Queenie said, narrowing her pale grey eyes.

"Marcus is a bit upset, that's all. Well, not upset, exactly, but worried."

"About his mother and father?" Queenie said, surprising her with her perception.

"Yes. But how did you know that?"

"I know it because I wasn't born yesterday, child. There's something going on in this house, and I'm not so daft that I can't see it as plain as day. And if you weren't in a daydream half the time, you'd probably have seen it too," Queenie said and laughed a little, seemingly trying to ease a little tension.

"But what is it? What's the matter with Mr and Mrs Daventry?"

"I don't know, but I've a feeling John knows something about it. You know what he's like, he's fearful nosy for a man!" John was the only other adult servant in the house.

The Daventry's were a good family, firmly placed in the middle classes, but not so wealthy that Mr Daventry could afford not to work, or Mrs Daventry could afford more than two live-in servants. As for Florence, she had never been paid. Of course, Mrs Daventry had never expected her to work, for she had come to the house with her Grandma as an orphaned child barely old enough to speak.

More than once, Queenie had told Florence how lucky they were to have found a position in a nice place like Wimbledon when Queenie was hardly in her first flush of youth and had her daughter's tiny child in tow. The Daventry's house had been a godsend, that's what Queenie had always said. Of course, the Daventrys likely thought that a hard-working woman, even if she was getting on a little in years, who was willing to work for very little beyond bed and board was every bit the godsend she thought them to be. Especially as her granddaughter was a free servant.

"Why don't you ask John about it, Grandma?"

"Because then he'll know that I want to know, and I can't have that."

"Why not?"

"Because he'll enjoy his little secrets then, and I won't give him the satisfaction."

"Anybody would think that you and John are sworn enemies, not friends. You tease each other worse than Marcus teases me."

"Ah, but I'm not head over heels in love with John Riley, I can assure you of that!" Queenie said and studied her granddaughter while she blushed. "I'm right, aren't I?"

"No, you're not right!" Florence said, her cheeks flaming.

"You're as red as a beetroot, girl! And as I said once before, I wasn't born yesterday. I was your age once, as hard as it might be for you to believe."

"Stop teasing me Gran," Florence said helplessly.

"Sorry, my sweet. But I know I'm right. I know I'm right as sure as I know that these feelings of yours won't do you any good. Much better you nip them in the bud before they become something that you can't manage."

"Can't manage?" Florence said, wondering what her Grandma really thought of such a thing now that the cat was out of the bag.

"I know you've known him all your life, Florence, but he is not for you. He's a nice young man, an impressive young man, and Mr and Mrs Daventry are far more kind and caring than many of their class, but they're still different. They're not *our* class, Florence, and we are not *theirs*. That's just the way the world works."

"I know it is, Grandma, I just wish it didn't. I don't understand why it has to be that way, really, I don't. Love should just be love, shouldn't it?"

"Probably, but it isn't. If you're going to be in love with somebody, let it be somebody who will be free to love you back. I'm not trying to upset you my sweet, I'm trying to save you from yourself. Encourage yourself in this, Florence, and you'll only be setting yourself up for sadness. I couldn't bear it, really I couldn't, not after your mother..." Suddenly, Queenie became tight-lipped. She had unwittingly spoken a thought out loud and Florence seized upon it.

"What about my mother?"

"We're not talking about your mother, Florence, we're talking about you."

"Did my mother fall in love with somebody she shouldn't have fallen in love with? Is that what you're trying to say?"

"I'm not trying to say anything, not about your mother." Queenie was getting annoyed, waspish.

Her grandmother always did this; whenever their conversation strayed into the details of the mother that Florence had never known, Queenie became evasive, even a little aggressive in her refusal to say much about her.

"Did my mother love my father?" Florence persisted, even though she knew exactly where this conversation was going to lead; nowhere. "And did he love her?"

"Where is any of this getting us, Florence? You're beginning to wear my last nerve with this, and I wish you wouldn't. It's a pointless conversation."

"Not to me, it isn't."

Queenie determinedly turned her attention to folding the pillowcases and stacking them neatly on top of the sheets in the linen cupboard. She would be quiet for the rest of the day, Florence knew that. But Queenie would forgive her granddaughter for her persistence, she always did.

Florence had no memory of her mother, and why would she? Gladys Smith had died giving birth to her, and Florence's memories had not begun before she and her grandmother had moved to Wimbledon to work in the home of Mr and Mrs Daventry. And as for Florence's father, Queenie never ever spoke of him. Florence didn't know if he was alive or dead, nor even what his name was. She had deduced, however, that since both she and her grandmother shared the surname of Smith, it was unlikely that her mother and father had ever been married. Of course, it wasn't something that she had ever asked Queenie about. There was only so far, she dared risk that formidable woman's wrath.

"Here, let me fold rest of the pillowcases, Grandma," Florence said, being the first to give in as always. Changing the subject, she let it be known that she wasn't going to ask any more questions about the parents she knew so little about.

Perhaps, in the end, a person ought only to concentrate on the relatives they had, not the relatives they didn't. Not to mention the fact that there was still the problem of Marcus. Well, not Marcus exactly, but Marcus' worries. Whatever they were, Florence hoped that they would be short-lived and, in the end, without consequence.

CHAPTER TWO

*A*s he stared out of the upstairs window at Florence, Marcus Daventry wondered just how much laundry there was to be done in a modest home such as theirs. Queenie and Florence seemed to be forever busy, and it was a constant source of silent shame to him that Florence had never been paid.

Of course, she wasn't considered an employee, but rather the dependant of one of their employees. Nonetheless, Marcus had seen how Florence had stepped in more and more to help her grandmother as that dear woman had begun to age. He only wished his mother would see it.

"Stephen, I do wish you would talk to me. If you

really have done this thing, I must know it. How can I help you otherwise?" His mother's anguished tone tore his attention away from his secret study of Florence Smith.

Marcus crept across the large Persian rug in his room until he reached the door. It was open just a little, enough for his mother's voice to have drifted through in the first place. Hearing his father's voice now, a lower, less anguished voice, Marcus strained to hear. Where were they? Their bedroom, surely. Marcus peered out through the gap, but the door to his parents' room was firmly closed. He held his breath before peering around the edge of the doorway, looking along the corridor toward the staircase. There they were, hovering at the top of the stairs, their heads close together as if in some secret conference.

"I wish you would believe me, Connie. If *you* do not, then why would anyone at Cooper and Soames?" There was an awful, heart-wrenchingly defeated tone to his father's voice which made Marcus' eyes fly wide open.

What on earth was happening? And what did it have to do with Cooper and Soames, the firm his father had worked for dealing in stocks and shares for years? Marcus finally let go of his breath, feeling light-headed as he wondered what on earth his mother suspected his father of. And whatever it was, it seemed that his colleagues at Cooper and Soames suspected it too. It gave him an awful sense of foreboding so overpowering that he couldn't bear it a moment longer.

Deciding not to listen to anything more, Marcus crossed back over the Persian rug to his spot by the window. He smiled when he saw her still there, pegging out the last of her laundry. Marcus knew this was a diversion. This was an avoidance of the most obvious kind, but he wanted to feel something different. He wanted to feel what he always felt when he looked at Florence.

But even his feelings for her had become a problem of late. He was seventeen now, almost a man, and Florence was just thirteen. It was as if the gap in their ages had widened as he'd become more of a man, leaving Florence wading alone through the warm pond of their shared childhood. Of course, Florence was smart, so clever, and hard working. Where was the child in amongst such qualities, such experience?

Florence, her last sheet hung out on the line, paused for a moment. Alone in the little yard used only for the work of the servants, she closed her eyes and tipped her head back, and he knew she was enjoying the feel of the early spring sunshine on her face. With the empty linen basket cradled in her arms, Florence remained that way for some time, and Marcus found himself hardly breathing again as if to do so would alert her to his presence and move her from that spot.

Marcus wanted to stare at her forever; he wanted to forget the niggling doubts which clawed at his mind with increasing regularity. He wanted to think only of that thick pale golden hair and those large, round blue eyes. He wanted to see only her dewy, youthful skin, her rosy lips.

So, why did he feel so bad? Perhaps because Marcus knew he was dreaming of something that could never be, not least because of what would undoubtedly be his parents' objections. Something else, however, was troubling him. Something bigger. Florence was four years younger than him, and he doubted that she was of an age to see him as anything other than the big brother figure who had played with her when they were young, and shared his tutor with her when the time came for him to learn to read and write before he went off to school.

Worse still, Marcus had an awful certainty that Florence would only ever see him that way. He was like family to her, the way she had been to him until just a few short weeks before. It had just happened one day, coming at him like a bolt from the blue. Nobody could have been more surprised than Marcus when he realised that the girl he'd always seen as a friend, a sister almost, now felt very different.

She was younger, yes, but he would wait for her. He'd wait as long as it took if there was even the smallest chance that the beautiful, funny, and clever Florence Smith might one day be his. And he would wait for her no matter what his mother and father thought.

Hearing his mother's unmistakable little footsteps fleeing down the stairs, Marcus knew that she was upset. He wanted to dash out to his father and ask him to be honest finally about whatever was happening in their world. But in the end, he couldn't tear himself away from the vision of the girl beyond the window; the girl who would probably never be his.

F lorence was waiting in the kitchen for her grandmother to return. She sat at the large square wooden table tracing her finger through the flour that Queenie had told her to clean up whilst she was gone. However, Florence couldn't concentrate, being certain that the strange cloud of worry which had hung over the house for so many weeks was about to bear rain.

Something had happened, Florence knew that with absolute certainty. She had only seen Marcus from afar in the last few days, but his ashen look had told its own story. Whatever had been troubling his parents was now known to him, she could almost feel it.

Queenie had been summoned to the drawing-room to speak to Mr and Mrs Daventry, Mr Daventry having arrived in the kitchen himself to make the request. It had all seemed so strange; Mrs Daventry was certainly no stranger to the kitchen, but Florence couldn't remember another time when Stephen

Daventry had graced that room. Something about that made this summons seem all the more serious, a little too real for Florence's liking.

When her grandmother finally returned almost half an hour later, the poor woman was ashen-faced, and Florence was certain she could detect a little redness around her eyes. Her own mouth went instantly dry; Queenie Smith was not the sort of woman who cried.

"Grandma? Grandma, what is it? What's happening?" Florence asked, immediately getting to her feet and settling her grandmother down in the chair she had just vacated.

"You were supposed to clean up this flour, Florence," Queenie said in a faraway voice as if she couldn't quite focus. "Not that it matters now, I suppose," she went on as Florence's heart began to pound uncomfortably.

"Forget about the flour, Gran," Florence said and could feel tears in her eyes. "Please, just tell me what's happening."

"Well, it looks like Mr Daventry has lost his job at Cooper and Soames," Queenie began, her voice wavering a little. She cleared her throat enthusiastically before continuing. "And so, we need to find somewhere else to live, my sweet."

"But why? Can't Mr Daventry get a job somewhere else?" Florence asked, almost breathless with the news.

"I said that myself, even though I know it's not my place to. Oh, but poor Mrs Daventry, she looks dreadful. When I asked if he couldn't simply get another job, she just bowed her head. I don't know what happened, but it seems it's serious."

"So, they can't afford to keep servants anymore?" Florence's voice didn't sound like her own.

"They can't afford to stay in London, Florence. Bedfordshire, that's where they're going. There be able to sell this place and get something cheaper, so Mr Daventry says. I suppose they'll have to live on whatever money they make from this house if Mr Daventry can't get another job."

"Can't we go with them, Grandma?" Florence was feeling desperate. She was terrified, of course, by the prospect of their sudden and unexpected situation. She was, however, more terrified of the prospect of being separated from the young man she was falling in love with. Surely Bedfordshire was a great distance from London, especially for Florence who had no means to make such a journey.

"No, Florence. It's just going to be the three of them. They'll be doing for themselves. They won't even have a manservant, not even a daily woman to waft a duster about the place. They're are in a terrible state."

"And I suppose we are in a terrible state too, then, aren't we? What are we going to do, Grandma? Where are we going to go?"

"Child, you're asking me questions I can't answer just now. You forget I've only had this news a few minutes longer than you have." Queenie had pulled herself together again and her slight waspishness was something of a relief. If Queenie fell apart, Florence knew that everything was lost.

"I know, I'm sorry. I just don't understand what could have gone so wrong."

"Well I know," John Riley strode into the kitchen seeming more intent on gossip than fear.

"Been listening at doors again, John?" Queenie said sarcastically, her face full of disapproval.

"Do you want to know what's happening or don't you? If you want to carry on sitting up there on your high horse, Queenie Smith, I'll leave you in ignorance." John adopted a ridiculously haughty air.

"I don't know why you're enjoying this so much, John Riley! It leaves you in as bad a position as it leaves us, doesn't it?"

"Not really, Queenie," John said and shrugged. "I'm younger than you, and I don't come with dependents, do I?" he said and nodded his head in Florence's direction. "I'll find myself a position soon enough, you see if I don't."

"John, don't speak to my grandmother like that," Florence said and scowled at him. "And it isn't a good thing to be so self-satisfied either."

"Oh, listen to you, Miss hoity-toity. Just because you grew up in this house doesn't mean you belong here, does it? Just because you got to learn to read and write and speak a bit different from the rest of us, doesn't make you any better."

"I didn't say that it did." Florence had never particularly liked John, but now she found herself despising him. "Why don't you just say what you came in here to stay? Why don't you just get it off your chest, spill the beans, like you've been itching to for weeks and weeks?"

"All right then," John said, the prospect of parting with a little gossip proving more of a draw than arguing was. "And you might not feel quite so sorry for poor Mr Daventry at the end of it." He was enjoying himself, and Florence wanted to kick him.

"Well?" Queenie snapped, losing patience.

"Turns out he did something dishonest at work, went against the company, he did."

"How?" Florence said, already refusing to believe it.

"I don't know all the ins and outs, something to do with those stocks and shares he buys and sells for that fancy company he worked for. Reckon he gave away some information to another firm, gave them a bit of an edge, and they made a killing out of it whilst Cooper and Soames made a loss."

"And just how would you know that?" Queenie said, shaking her head and rolling her eyes.

"I heard him and Mrs Daventry talking about it. She was asking him if it was true, and he was moaning his head off because his own wife doesn't trust him. But there's no smoke without fire, is there? That's what I always say!"

"You sound as if you want it to be true, John," Florence said, shaking her head. "What has Mr Daventry ever done to you?"

"They're all as bad as each other, them lot," he said and pushed his nose up with his forefinger to indicate snobbery. "I don't see why I should care about any of them. I work my fingers to the bone for these people and for what?"

"John Riley, the next time you work your fingers to the bone will be the first time. You ought to be grateful you kept a position here for so long." Queenie was shaking her head and glaring at him. "You've been earning money for old rope these last few years, anybody else would have cast you out on your ear. Good luck keeping a position anywhere else unless you buck your ideas up, that's what I say."

"Good luck finding a position anywhere at your age, Queenie Smith. Reckon the only way you'll be able to survive your old age will be to turn that one out to work on the streets, peddling her wares when the sailors come to town!" Before he had finished his sentence, Queenie was on her feet.

She advanced upon him, and Florence gasped when she realised her grandmother had lifted the rolling pin from the table.

"Gran!" Florence squealed, suddenly afraid.

"All right, Queenie, it was just a joke!" John said, backing away across the kitchen and clearly as stunned as Florence was that Queenie had taken his poorly judged comment so badly.

"Hateful words like that ain't a joke to me, John Riley. You mind yourself these last couple of weeks in this house. You mind you stay out of my way, or you'll feel this rolling pin across the side of your head, do you hear me?" Florence had never seen her grandmother so furious in all her life.

It was an insult, of course it was, but Queenie ordinarily sported a much thicker skin. Something about her grandmother's reaction gave Florence the sense that all was not as it seemed.

"Why don't you take yourself off into the yard, John?" Florence said, wanting to bring this uncertain and uncomfortable moment to an end.

As John made his exit, Florence gently took the rolling pin from her grandmother's hand and led her back to the table. This had been a terrible day full of terrible news, and she could only imagine that it was this which had made Queenie suddenly volatile.

"I'm sorry about that, child," Queenie said and sniffed loudly.

"It's all right Grandma, you've had a horrible shock today. We just need to work out what we're going to do next, that's all. We'll be all right, I promise." Even as she spoke the words, Florence had the awful feeling that they most certainly would not be all right.

CHAPTER THREE

"I don't think I've ever been to Limehouse, Florence," Marcus said as the two of them leaned against the back wall of the house. It was a warm day, a full spring day, complete with blue sky and singing birds and a warm and gentle breeze. It was so at odds with everything that Florence was feeling that she could have wished the heavens to open and let the falling rain suit her mood.

"I haven't been to Limehouse before either, Marcus. I don't expect it's very nice. It won't be a good part of London like Wimbledon is." Her voice sounded riddled with exhaustion, she was so defeated.

"And Queenie's found you somewhere, has she?

Somewhere nice?" Marcus asked, his voice full of caring and hope. It was as if he needed to know that Florence and her grandmother would be all right, that they would be safe and happy. If only Florence could give that to him, but she couldn't.

"I haven't seen it myself, Marcus. It's just a room in a tenement building. As much as Grandma will tell me is that it will keep the rain off us. You know what she's like, she won't dress something up to be pretty if it's anything but."

"I wish there was something I could do. I just wish that none of this had ever happened, that the people at Cooper and Soames hadn't been so ready to believe my father could be dishonest."

"I don't believe it," Florence said, and almost reached out her hand. But as always, something stopped her. If only she had just a little bit more experience of the world or at least an understanding of how these things were supposed to go.

"You're the only one who doesn't believe it. Everybody else is looking at my family as if we committed some sort of awful crime. My father's friends have all turned their backs on him, my mother's friends won't give her a kind word or offer her any comfort at all."

"Then they were never friends in the first place. A real friend remains a friend no matter what has happened."

"Like us?" Marcus turned his dark head, his bright blue eyes fixing on hers.

"Yes, just like us, Marcus."

"I will miss seeing you every day. You've been here almost as long as I have," he said and laughed sadly. You know, I can still just about remember the day you came here with Queenie."

"Can you really?" Florence asked, surprised. He'd never said this before, and he must surely have been so young himself at the time.

"You were so adorable running around the place. I think my mother took such a liking to you that she employed Queenie without a second thought." His smile was so handsome, so real.

"I can't have been running around the place, Marcus, I was only a baby."

"No, not quite a baby," he said and stared off across the yard as if looking into the past. "You had a sweet little dress on, and the tiniest boots I'd ever seen. I think it's the little boots I remember more than anything."

"Really?" Florence said, feeling confused. As far as she was concerned, she'd been no more than a babe in arms when Queenie had found the position in Wimbledon. Perhaps she had misunderstood, or perhaps Marcus was just remembering things a little differently from how they had really been.

"I can't bear this," he said. "I haven't even seen the house in Bedfordshire, I didn't want to see it. I want to be here, it's my home. I want to be here, and I want you to be here and I want Queenie to be here. I know I sound like a petulant child, but this is too much to bear."

This was their last day at the house in Wimbledon. The following morning, with everything packed up and moved out, they would be going their separate ways; Marcus and his family to Bedfordshire, and Florence and Queenie to Limehouse. He was right; it really was too much to bear.

"I'll miss you, Marcus," Florence said, her cheeks blushing as her confidence waned. "You've always been in my life."

"Like a big brother?" he said, looking at the floor.

"Yes, I suppose so," Florence said, but she didn't mean it. Her heart wanted to tell him that it wasn't how she viewed him anymore, but she didn't know where to begin. This was their last day together, and she didn't want him to be horrified by her childish crush on him. She didn't want her last memory of him to be a look of rejection.

"Everything comes to an end, doesn't it?" he said, his voice so full of melancholy that Florence struggled to hold back her tears. "Even happiness."

"Try to hold onto the happiness you felt here, Marcus. I know I will. Nothing will ever compare to this, not in my life, and my memories of this house, this family, are so precious to me. I'll let them sustain me through the dark times, and you should try to do the same."

"How did you get to be so clever?"

"Because you let me sit at your side and learn when

you were learning," she said. "I know what I owe your family, all of you, and I just wish that there was something I could do now to make this better."

"What will I do without you, my dear?" Marcus looked into her eyes again, and this time Florence couldn't hold back her tears. "Come here," he said, and wrapped his arms around her, drawing her towards him.

Florence leaned against him, almost dissolving into him. They had never embraced before, not even when they were younger, and it was so wonderful and so desperately sad all at once that she didn't know which way was up. He was so tall, his arms feeling like a protective barrier that was keeping the world out, the world, and all its woes.

Florence cried and cried into the rough fabric of his waistcoat, her own arms wrapped around his back, clinging on tightly. She never ever wanted to let go.

"One day, we'll be friends again. One day, all this awfulness will be over, and everything will be all right again. I promise you it will, Florence. I promise you," he whispered the words into her hair.

If only she could tell him how she felt. If only she

could say the words which would let him know that her heart had room only for him. But she was just a girl, and he almost a man. It seemed her fear would always hold her back.

When they finally broke their embrace, Florence dried her eyes on the handkerchief he gave her. She looked up at him, and he smiled down at her sadly. Finally, he kissed her, but he kissed her cheek. If ever there was a gesture from brother to sister, Florence knew it was that. If he felt for her what she felt for him, surely, he would have kissed her lips. She knew enough of the world to know that *that* was how it worked.

And now, on top of all her sadness, Florence Smith added her heartbreak.

As the post carriage bore them through the streets of London, Florence felt numb. She had lain awake all night dreading the moment when she would walk away from the house in Wimbledon, from everything she had ever known. From Marcus.

Florence and her grandmother had a surprising amount of possessions given their station in life, and they would never have made it on foot from Wimbledon to Limehouse carrying their things. Mr Daventry had insisted upon paying their carriage fair, on top of the severance pay that he had been kind enough to give to Queenie.

Florence didn't care what John Riley said about *their sort*. The Daventrys had been different, and only a fool wouldn't have seen it. In the midst of their own nightmare, they had parted with much-needed money so that their loyal servant and her granddaughter could survive for a few weeks, giving them time to find new jobs and positions. It made her sad and grateful all at once.

"Is this it, Grandma?" Florence asked, her face pressed against the window of the carriage as she looked out onto the misery. The houses were blackened, marred by soot, and every window was a filthy, unseeing eye onto the world.

"No, we're not there yet," Queenie said, but there was something about the way she had looked out, her face suddenly pale, that had given Florence to understand that they had arrived.

"But where is this?" Florence asked, not ready to let it go. "If this isn't Limehouse, where is it?"

"Whitechapel," Queenie said, her tone suggesting that she would say no more about it. She looked away from the window, studying her hands in her lap, keeping her own counsel.

Florence was used to Queenie's evasive ways; she'd been that way for as long as Florence could remember. Quite what she had to be evasive about Florence had never understood, but she had long since stopped hoping that she would ever get to the bottom of things. Now that she was older, she had developed a greater sense that there really was something to get to the bottom of, she just couldn't imagine what.

"It doesn't look like a very nice place, Grandma."

"It isn't."

"Is Limehouse better?" Florence asked with some determination.

"It is as far as I'm concerned," Queenie said, cryptically.

In just a matter of minutes, the post carriage drew up

and the driver shouted down. Florence couldn't make out his words, but she knew instinctively that they had finally arrived in Limehouse, an instinct that was confirmed when she felt the carriage rock from side to side as the driver jumped down to help them out with their things.

As far as Florence could see, Limehouse looked no different from Whitechapel. She couldn't understand why Queenie thought it a better place, for Florence hadn't seen any discernible break between the two. It looked like one big place, sprawling and dark and miserable. She closed her eyes for a moment and longed for the wide-open space on Wimbledon Common, that lush green grass, that clean air. It was only a few miles away, and yet it was as if there were two very different Londons, as remote from one another as far-flung countries.

The driver opened the door and helped Queenie down, leaving Florence to jump out herself. In no time at all, he'd kindly carried their wooden trunks to a large and blackened tenement building. It seemed to Florence that the very air was thick with industry, with soot, with the very obvious signs of hard work and hard lives plain to see.

The streets were narrow, and the buildings were low. It felt like a rabbit warren, only nowhere near as pleasant. Even though the sun was shining, it was as if it couldn't make its way through the thick air to touch the streets below.

It seemed noisy, voices everywhere, hurrying feet, shouts, one million conversations. Florence felt overwhelmed by it, looking all around her at huddles of ragged-looking children furtively searching for some chance which might mean they ate that day. She had heard of such children, of the ones so poor they had no option but to steal, and now she wondered if she was about to join their ranks. If there was work to be had here in Limehouse, why did it look so impoverished?

Her heart didn't leap any higher when they were finally inside the room that was to be their home from now on. It was a large room, but there was almost nothing in it. There was a bed that looked as if its best days were behind it, and she was glad that Mrs Daventry had given them plenty of sheets so that they might cover the ugly markings on the mattress.

There was a fireplace, at least, and she was glad that she would be able to keep her grandmother warm if nothing else. The room was dark, despite the huge ground floor window which gave out onto a yard beyond. But therein lay the problem; the wall around that yard was built higher than the windows, surely blocking the light for much of the day.

There was no stove, but there was a metal tripod and some hooks; they would have to hang their pots and pans over the open fire to cook. This was a different world, a far cry from the bright and welcoming kitchen in Wimbledon. Even having seen the poorest of them outside on the street, still, this felt like true poverty. How was she ever to get used to this?

"As I said, Florence, it'll keep the rain off. We are all right for a while, and we've got more than most. If you set your mind to it, you can get used to anything."

"I know, Grandma," Florence said in as bright a voice as she could muster. "And look, we have a table and chairs. We have somewhere to sit, haven't we?" she continued in her bright manner, determined not to let Queenie see just how low she felt. After all, her grandmother was, as always, doing her very best for her. They had each other, and as Queenie has said, they had more than most.

"And I'll find myself a position soon enough, you see if I don't. Don't forget, I have a wonderful reference from Mrs Daventry. Things will be back to normal in no time."

Queenie's words unsettled her, for her grandmother really wasn't the sort of person who sugar-coated anything. But this was sugar-coating, without a doubt. Florence could see in her eyes that her grandmother didn't really hold out much hope of finding a position in service. But this was no time for Florence to give in to her fears. It was time for her to look out for the grandmother who had looked out for her for her entire life.

"We will both find positions, Grandma. We're going to be just fine." Even as she spoke, Florence was fighting her tears.

CHAPTER FOUR

"Just be glad you're not a little kid, Flo or Mr Mason would have you nipping in between the machinery to pick the fluff out." Jenny, the girl who worked in the textile mill beside her, was sometimes pleasant but usually obnoxious.

"Yes, it looks so dangerous." Florence had her eyes fixed on a small and skinny little girl whose nimble fingers worked quickly to pick out the fluff and loose threads which had choked the loom. "And they are all so young."

"Not all of them," Jenny said, her obnoxious tone returning. "Enough of them are your age, believe me.

It's just that they ain't been fed as well as you have, that's all."

"Is that right?" Florence gritted her teeth, determined to avoid an argument that would see Mr Mason throw her out of her job in a heartbeat.

"I reckon your sort eat better in Wimbledon, don't they?" Jenny was goading her.

Florence fixed her eyes on the little girl wedged inside the loom, praying she would get out safely. Jenny was looking for an argument, and Florence had decided not to give her one.

"And I heard Mr Mason saying you can read and write and all. I expect you think yourself quite high-minded, don't you?"

"Not standing here I don't," Florence said sarcastically. "You'd better get on with your work and stop talking, Jenny, Mr Mason is coming."

Jenny looked set to say more, but Mr Mason was indeed making his way down along the line of looms, his dark beady eyes flicking this way and that in search of some misdemeanour he could make much of. He was a hateful creature, and after only three weeks in her job, Florence already despised him.

She had despised him from the very beginning, from their first meeting, when he had laughed in Queenie's face at the idea that she would manage a twelve-hour day working at one of the looms. He told her she was too old, that the master didn't give out money for nothing. When Florence had been about to object, to tell him what she thought of him, Queenie had squeezed her hand, her eyes beseeching her to do nothing of the sort. They needed one of them to be earning, for the money that Mr Daventry had given them would not last forever.

And so it was that Florence had bit down on her tongue and kept her feelings about Mr Mason to herself. The three weeks she had worked at the textile mill just a short walk from Limehouse had been the longest three weeks of her life. She'd always been a hard worker, never hiding herself away when there was something to be done, but she had enjoyed her work before. She had enjoyed hanging out the laundry, folding sheets, keeping the neat and cosy drawing-room at the house in Wimbledon smart and dust-free. But this was different; there was no satisfaction in it, no obvious end result barring great roles of plain, utilitarian fabric. It wasn't even a pleasant colour, just a horrible dirty sort of cream. She couldn't begin to imagine what would be made out of such stuff.

"Don't bother trying to be Mr Mason's pet, Flo," Jenny said in a hiss as soon as the danger of his beady eyes had passed. "He doesn't have pets. He hates everybody, he doesn't even get upset when one of the little ones get squashed to death between the looms." The casual way in which Jenny talked about death made Florence shudder.

"I don't want to be anybody's pet," Florence hissed back waspishly. "My name is *Florence*, not Flo."

"Ooh-ooh-ooh," Jenny said, mocking her.

"Jenny, if you continue to irritate me, I will speak to Mr Mason about it. I'll tell him I can't concentrate on my work with you always talking, he won't be happy about that, will he?"

"And I'll tell everybody that you're a snide!"

"What makes you think I care what anybody else thinks of me?" Florence was a mild-mannered girl, but she knew how to stick up for herself and she'd had just about enough of the angry, greasy, malodorous Jenny. She was pernicious, trying to hurt needlessly, being cruel and spiteful just for its own sake.

"You wouldn't! You wouldn't dare!" Jenny said, trying to sound confident, but her vacant, pale green eyes told a different story. She wasn't so sure.

Florence turned square on to Jenny, staring at her, getting ready to take her on for the first time. As much as she was trying to avoid an argument, she knew that if she didn't stop this in its tracks, it would just continue day after day. It would make her life working in the mill worse, it was going to be miserable enough without such nonsense as that. Florence didn't speak for the longest time, and Jenny, horribly thin and angular, began to look uncomfortable.

Without another word, Florence turned away and took a step, a step in the direction of Mr Mason. Jenny reached out and seized her wrist, clinging on to her, her eyes silently begging Florence not to give her away.

"I don't want to get you into trouble, Jenny. But

understand this; if you keep goading me, I won't think twice. I don't care what you think about me, what you think about my life before I ended up here, it just isn't important. What is important is that I find some way to get through each day, and listening to you being unnecessarily picky and spiteful does not form a part of that plan, do you understand me?" Florence became aware of some interest in their conversation from some of the other young women, and even more aware that they seemed a little in awe of her. After three weeks in that place, it was certainly the last thing that she expected.

"All right, all right, don't get your knickers in a twist," Jenny said and rolled her eyes, but her capitulation was as obvious as the long and pointed nose on her face.

Jenny turned back to her work, and Florence did the same. She was pleased to note that the rest of the day went along much better without Jenny's perpetual barbs, and she was glad that she had stood up for herself in the end. The only problem was, without Jenny to contend with, Florence had more time to think.

She couldn't help wondering if life would ever

improve. If there would ever be more to it than simply turning up every day at the mill and doing the same things over and over again for so little money that it didn't even cover the rent on that awful room she shared with her grandmother. Things might have been easier had Mr Mason not been so unbending if he had taken Queenie on as well. However, the work was hard, and the hours were long, and so much time was spent standing in one place that Florence knew her grandmother's ageing legs wouldn't have supported her through it.

Even back in Wimbledon, Florence had taken on more and more work, of course then she was happy to do so, content to think that she and Queenie would be there forever. But what would become of them now? Already Queenie was talking about brewing her own gin and selling it, but Florence could hardly think about such a thing without worrying.

Perhaps the peelers would catch her, perhaps she would end up in dreadful trouble. Florence shook her head; *the peelers*. Nobody in Wimbledon described the police in such a way, but *the peelers* seemed to be all that anybody here in Limehouse talked about. There were a lot more of them, too, likely because Limehouse and the little places that surrounded it were just the sorts of places in which they were needed. Crime was everywhere, and she couldn't bear to think of her grandmother joining in, even if it were out of necessity.

Of course, in a place like Limehouse, there was always a market for it. Queenie seemed quite unperturbed by the idea, and Florence realised that this wasn't new to her. Her grandmother had begun in a place like this, not like Florence who had begun in a place like Wimbledon.

However necessary it all might be in the end, Florence was certain that she would never, ever get used to it.

"I only want to say hello, Miss snooty!" The young man who had been hovering outside the mill for the better part of a week wandered along behind Florence as she made her way home.

"Miss snooty?" Florence said, turning on her heel to glare at him, speaking to him for the first time. "I'm getting a little tired of people here in Limehouse thinking they know me." And she really had had enough of it. She wasn't going to squash Jenny only to let this overly confident young man take her place.

"I didn't really mean it, I just wanted to say something that would make you speak at last," the young man said and smiled brightly at her. "I'm glad I risked it; you've got a proper nice voice."

"Well, thank you," Florence said in a flat tone before turning away.

"You're not from round 'ere, are you?" he asked, suddenly keeping step with her, walking along at her side. How she longed for the peace of her old life.

"No, I'm not," Florence was exasperated; she wanted this conversation to end.

"Wimbledon, somebody said," he went on, his voice rising at the end of his sentence, a voluble question mark.

"Yes, Wimbledon."

"You're not the chattiest of girls, are you?"

"No."

"Blimey, you're hard work!" the young man said and burst out laughing.

Florence stopped walking for a moment, finding a smile begrudgingly spread across her face. The young man's laugh was so pleasant, so amused, and without a hint of the scorn and cruelty that she'd heard in other people's laughter since she'd been living in Limehouse. There wasn't the same unsettling cynicism in it.

"That's better! Blimey, you've got a pretty smile."

"Well, I'm sure that a pretty smile doesn't get you far in life," Florence said and looked back over her shoulder towards the textile mill.

"I wouldn't be so sure of that," the young man said and laughed. "I'm Jimmy, by the way." He thrust a hand out, and she was relieved to see that it was clean. She took his hand without hesitation and shook it. No wonder everybody thought her so prim and proper; she'd have to get used to the way things were now, she knew that.

"I'm Florence."

"It's nice to meet you, Flo," he said, his face made all the more handsome by the broad grin.

"No, not Flo, *Florence*." She shrugged her shoulders. "And I don't care if that makes me hoity-toity or snooty, it's just the way it is."

"I like a girl who knows how to stick up for herself, *Florence*," he said, laying heavy emphasis on her name. "And I don't blame you either. Florence is a pretty name, the sort of name that should be said all the way from one end to the other. All right then, Florence it is." He nodded, and his thick dark hair fell down over his eyes.

He swept his hair back in a gesture that she knew must surely be habitual, and she noted his eyes. His hair was as dark as Marcus Daventry's, and his eyes were blue, but a very different blue. They were the palest blue she'd ever seen, a disconcertingly washed-out version of Marcus' eyes. They weren't unpleasant, just curiously disturbing. If she honest, Florence didn't know if it was a good sort of disturbing or a bad sort of disturbing. Perhaps only time would tell.

"I suppose I'm getting used to sticking up for myself

working in that place," Florence said and began to walk slowly, silently letting Jimmy know that he was quite welcome to continue to walk beside her. "It's awful."

"I suppose you get a really good slice of society in there, Florence. Folk round 'ere is hard, make no mistake about it, and places like that," he said, looking over his shoulder at the textile mill just as Florence had done moments before. "Places like that thrive on the poverty and the misery, the desperation and the need. Bet they don't pay much, do they?"

"Not enough for me to look after my grandmother properly, no," Florence said, feeling a strange sense of relief to be able to talk about it at last. She'd kept her fears to herself at home, not wanting Queenie to feel responsible for their circumstances. After all, Queenie wasn't responsible. This was just life; Florence was beginning to learn that now.

"I reckon a girl like you will pick up something better soon enough. You seem smart enough, and you've got that pretty face of yours. Don't be downhearted by it."

"Thank you," Florence said and smiled at him

sheepishly. "I'm sorry I ignored you for so many days. I'm struggling to find my place here in Limehouse. The truth is, I don't think I really have one."

"In the end, we all fit in everywhere. You don't have to be just the same as everybody else to find your place, you just have to be comfortable, that's all."

"Be comfortable to be *miss snooty* in a place like Limehouse?" Florence teased, and it reminded her a little of the wonderful conversations she used to share with Marcus. Those hazy, sunny days when they had teased one another as she had hung rows of sheets out on the line. It made her eyes suddenly fill with tears.

"I don't really think you're snooty at all, Florence. As I said, I was just trying to get your attention and I don't reckon I'm quite as bright as you to find a better way of doing it. You *are* different, though. You stand out." He surprised her by reaching out to gently pat her hand before withdrawing his and sliding it into his pocket.

"I'm not sure standing out is such a good thing here in Limehouse."

"Well, I reckon it is. You stand out for being clean and decent and gentle, even if you have got a sharp tongue and you can stand up for yourself," he added the last with a laugh. "Are you crying?" He looked genuinely concerned.

"No, not quite." She blinked hard, dispelling the tears in her eyes.

"Just because they haven't fallen, doesn't mean you're not crying. I mean, you feel like crying, so how is it any better not to?"

"You're quite persistent, aren't you?" Florence said and laughed, giving in and rubbing at her eyes with her fists.

"I'm just about the most persistent man in all of Limehouse," he said, grinning at her again, although she could see that concern still hovering. He was an unusual young man, sounding rougher than he looked, and being kinder and gentler than he appeared. He seemed to be a mixture of contrasts, and already he was the most interesting person Florence had met since leaving Wimbledon behind.

"And does persistence do well for you?"

"I manage," he said and shrugged.

"What do you do?"

"A little bit of this and a little bit of that. I seize whatever work opportunities come my way and I get by. I get by all right, really." He was tall, like Marcus, although not perhaps quite as tall.

He seemed to Florence to be about the same age, seventeen or eighteen, certainly no more. He had that same appearance of transition that Marcus had, the boy who was becoming a man. She realised that there was something reassuring about it, something almost unique. A young man of that age was manly enough to have confidence in and yet young enough to be confident with. Somehow, she didn't feel like quite the child she had felt in Marcus' presence, although she had a firm idea that her new circumstances had much to do with it.

Life was hard and harsh, and she had learned so much about it in the few weeks since she had last seen Marcus. Would she have been different with him now? Would she have been able to say the things she wanted to say that final day as they had stood in the yard leaning against the back of the house? She thought she probably would. The knowledge gave her no comfort, rather it made her feel sadder than she had ever felt. But for the sake of a few weeks, she had wasted her opportunity, to be honest. Just another one of life's cruel twists, she gathered.

"You're obviously not working now if you're able to hover about outside the textile mill day after day," Florence said, deciding to tease him a little to take the edge off her own sadness.

"Ah, but my working day is just about to begin," Jimmy said and chuckled. "Limehouse is the sort of place that never sleeps and there's always something happening, day or night."

"And you don't mind working at night?"

"I don't mind at all as long as there's a little bit of money at the end of it. A way to survive." As she studied him, she realised that this young man perhaps fared a little better than others.

His clothes were old, but they were well kept, and she had a feeling that they had been well made in the beginning. She had no doubt that they had once belonged to somebody else, but Jimmy would have needed to part with some hard-earned money to procure them in the first place. The material of his trousers was thick and dark grey. He wore a waistcoat over the top of his shirt and, whilst it didn't quite match the trousers, the two fabrics weren't entirely dissimilar.

He had collars clipped to his white shirt, something which so many other men in Limehouse didn't seem to bother with. The collars had seen better days, but still, it made him look curiously smart. He didn't wear a jacket, but she had the feeling that he very likely possessed one. It was still a warm day, spring was turning into summer, and he had the sleeves of his shirt rolled up to the elbow, exposing tanned and muscular forearms. His arms and hands made him look like even more of a man, and she found herself staring at them for a moment. There was something about this new friend of hers which made her feel a little more secure as if there might be some other chances in life after all.

"Have you always lived in Limehouse, Jimmy?" Florence asked gently, turning her attention from his masculine hands.

"More or less. I mean I was born and started off my life over in Whitechapel, but since it's a stone's throw, I don't suppose I've come very far," he said and laughed again, that wonderful light laugh that had caused her to speak to him in the first place. "What about you? Were you born in Wimbledon?" he went on conversationally.

"I... actually, I don't know," Florence said, feeling a little embarrassed. "My Grandma doesn't talk about it much. My mother died when I was born, and I suppose that's when my Grandma moved us over to Wimbledon. But honestly, I don't know. I don't like to ask questions about those times, it makes her so sad."

"The poor old duck, that *is* sad. And sad for you too, Florence, never knowing your mother, I mean."

"Is your mother still alive?"

"No, not anymore, but at least I have some memories of her."

"And your father?"

"Long gone," Jimmy said, and those impossibly pale blue eyes seemed to darken before he looked down at the grey pavement. Florence decided not to push it any further. She wanted to know where he lived, who he lived with, but she suddenly had the greatest sense that she would be prying, somehow picking at an old sore.

"Well, this is where I leave you, Jimmy," Florence said, drawing to a halt outside the tenement building. "And this is where I live with my Grandma," she added, feeling very much less secretive and guarded than she had done just minutes before. It felt good to open up, to unfurl, as it were, from the tight shell she had been constructing from the moment she'd arrived in Limehouse.

"Which door is it?" he asked without any hint of embarrassment at his own prying.

"That one there, the one that's barely clinging to the frame," Florence said humorously, and Jimmy laughed.

"You have a good evening, Florence. And who knows, maybe I'll be waiting for you tomorrow outside the mill. Maybe I'll walk you home again, what do you say to that?" He was smiling at her and his handsomeness, his attractiveness, was undeniable. He wasn't Marcus Daventry, for nobody was, but in her lonely world, this pale-eyed young man presented something of a bright spot on the horizon. A bright spot that Florence wasn't about to turn her back on.

"I suppose I'd say *I'll see you tomorrow*," Florence said, doing a little grinning of her own.

"Right," Jimmy said and nodded, his face full of surprise; he'd expected her to turn him down flat. "Well, I'll see you tomorrow, Florence."

CHAPTER FIVE

Queenie walked through the dark and narrow corridor which led from the back of the house where their own room was, to the front. She opened the door just a crack and peered out into the street beyond. Queenie didn't want her granddaughter to see her spying, but she had a feeling that something had changed of late. She knew girls of that age as well as she knew herself. After all, she hadn't just raised her granddaughter, but her own daughter and she could spot the little signs of romance at a hundred yards.

She knew she was being overprotective; Florence had turned fourteen now after all, and if she was honest, it was probably time that the girl had something nice in her life. This had been a year of loss for her, and a little happiness and excitement could go a long way to making her feel better. But it could always go too far, and it chilled Queenie to the bone just to think about it.

This wasn't Wimbledon, this was Limehouse. This was a stone's throw from Whitechapel, that place of misery where the same story was told over and over again, the only thing changing being the name of the young girl in question. Well, she wanted better than that for Florence. She wanted her to have a life, to have some chances, and getting herself in the family way would certainly put paid to that.

"Queenie, do you always have to expect the worst?" she whispered to herself and laughed, her laughter quickly turning into that horrible dry cough which had been plaguing her for so long now.

For a moment, Queenie had to brace herself against the wall of the narrow entrance while she coughed and coughed, always trying to clear something that never seemed to move. It was irritating and debilitating once the cough took hold of her. It seemed pointless trying to shift something from her lungs that seemed never to move, but it was irresistible somehow, and the cough came about of its own accord and left of its own accord. By the time Queenie had recovered from her coughing fit, Florence was already walking along the street.

Queenie pushed the door further closed, leaving herself only a tiny gap to peer out through. It was a good thing that she still had good eyesight, especially at her age when everything else seemed to be already well worn and long past its best.

"Aha, I knew it," Queenie whispered to herself and began to chuckle. There, ambling along at Florence's side, was a young man. He looked to be about the same age as Marcus Daventry, and he had that dark hair too. No wonder Florence had seemed just a little brighter of late. The poor girl had been so down, so heartbroken, having to give up her first love before it had even begun.

Despite her misgivings, despite her fears for Florence's future, didn't the girl deserve this? Didn't she deserve this bright corner to turn into?

Knowing that she would be seen if she hovered at the door for much longer, Queenie let out a great sigh. She was about to turn when the young man, a little clearer now that he was closer, turned his head in a particular way to look at Florence. It almost made Queenie's heart stop. It was so familiar as if it were a sight she had seen just yesterday.

She realised then just how much Florence looked like her mother. Gladys had had the same pale golden hair, the same slim but substantial frame. And that man, that young man, it was almost as if Warren Bates himself had risen from the grave. Queenie wasn't watching Florence and some anonymous young man anymore, she was staring down the years, staring at Gladys walking along at the side of Warren Bates. Nothing would force her away from that door now, and as her granddaughter drew ever closer, Queenie was determined to have a better look at that young man.

"Florence?" Queenie called out, trying to sound normal, smiling even, wanting her to bring the young man closer still.

"Grandma, what are you doing by the door?"

Florence asked and started to laugh in that gentle, melodic way of hers.

"I thought I'd greet you, my sweet. There's nothing wrong with that, is there?" Although Queenie was trying to sound like her normal self, her heart was thundering and her voice sounded higher in pitch, a little strained. Florence must have noticed it too, for she was looking at Queenie through narrowed eyes, her eyebrows raised a little in question.

"Nothing at all, Grandma." Florence was still studying her, and now Queenie wasn't the only one who was trying to appear normal. "This is a friend of mine, Jimmy," she went on, flushing a little as the young man at her side moved awkwardly from foot to foot.

"Hello, Jimmy," Queenie said, and finally looked the young man full in the face. He was just a few feet away from her now, there could be no mistake.

That hair was dark and thick, just like Warren Bates' had been. He was tall and looked strong, but then so did plenty of young men, didn't they? It was the eyes, in the end, which told Queenie that she was right. She had never seen such pale blue eyes before. The pupils looked almost terrifyingly dark set against such an insipid surrounding. They were wide eyes too, round, unmistakable.

"Hello, Mrs Smith," Jimmy said politely, and something about his friendly manner almost took her off guard. But then Warren Bates had had a friendly manner when he wanted, didn't he? The man had been a chameleon, and Queenie knew right down to her very bone marrow that this young man was exactly the same. She felt suddenly hot and sick, old images coming back to her with such clarity it was as if no time at all had passed.

"Grandma, are you all right?" Florence hurried down the path and reached out to take Queenie's hand. "You look as white as a sheet."

Queenie knew she was as white as a sheet; she'd felt the blood drain from her face as it was happening, an almost physical sensation. This young man could only be the son of Warren Bates. Not a nephew, not a second cousin, but that man's son. He was like him in every detail, the sort of likeness that only a parent and child could share. Queenie's throat began to spasm, and she had the awful feeling that she would be sick.

"I'm just having a turn, my dear," Queenie said, trying to waft away her granddaughter's concerns with a frail hand. She couldn't take her eyes off Jimmy, and the young man was beginning to wilt a little beneath her determined study of him.

"Come on, let's get you inside," Florence said, seeming a little flustered and turning to look apologetically at Jimmy.

"Is there anything I can do?" Jimmy asked, taking a couple of steps towards them. However, Queenie held out her hand much more firmly this time and shook her head.

"No thank you, young man," Queenie said, her tone gentle but her eyes steely. She stared directly into those pale blue orbs, trying to silently give that young man the message that he must never, ever darken their door again. "We'll be perfectly all right, won't we, Florence?" Queenie was trying to make this right, to be normal for Florence's benefit.

"Well, if you're sure," Jimmy said and shrugged awkwardly. "It was nice to meet you, Mrs Smith. I'll see you later, Florence," he said, and Queenie watched as he turned his attention to her granddaughter. He smiled at her, that slow, appealing smile that his father had always used to such great effect on Queenie's beloved Gladys.

"Thank you, Jimmy," Florence said, and Queenie could have cried out in dismay when she saw Florence's cheeks flush. So, she liked this boy.

As Florence helped her back into their room, Queenie had the awful sensation of history repeating itself.

"**A**re you sure you're all right, Grandma?" Florence said, fussing, sitting her grandmother down on the edge of the bed in case she needed to lay down.

"I'm all right, I'm all right," Queenie said, breathing slowly and determinedly, the way she always breathed when she was hoping that a coughing fit wouldn't seize her.

"I think you need a doctor, Grandma."

"We don't have money to be wasting on doctors,

Florence. And in any case, there's nothing wrong with me."

"Nothing wrong with you? I'd never seen you look so white. You're sick, Gran," Florence said and felt her throat tightening with emotion. She wanted to cry, but Queenie didn't really like that sort of thing.

"There's nothing wrong with me that never setting eyes on that boy again won't cure."

"What?" Florence said, her mouth falling open; of all the things she had expected her grandmother to say, that was not among them. "What do you mean? What did Jimmy do wrong?"

"Oh, nothing. Don't mind me, my sweet. I've had a turn and I'm lashing out. Don't take it to heart now, will you?" Queenie's face softened, but it was a very determined sort of a softening as if she was struggling with it.

"I don't understand."

"Oh, you will, when you get as old as I am. You'll get obstinate and gnarly and say things you don't mean, believe me. No, don't you go taking it to heart," Queenie said, the colour seeming to return to her cheeks at last. "I shouldn't have said that. I shouldn't have taken it out on that young man. Young Jimmy..." Queenie said, and her brow wrinkled as she looked up at Florence. Jimmy *what?* What did you say his name was?"

"Jimmy," Florence said and shrugged. "Just Jimmy. I don't know his surname."

"You haven't been friends for long then?" Queenie's tone had changed entirely into something that was more wheedling, the sort of tone that fished for information.

"Just a few weeks really, that's all. I've only seen him a few times, it's not what you think it is," Florence said, but she could feel her cheeks blushing again. "I mean he just walks me along the street sometimes when I come out of the mill and head for home."

"He works at the mill then, does he?" If Florence didn't know better, she'd think that her grandmother looked curiously hopeful.

"No, he doesn't work at the mill, I've just seen him outside a few times."

"What does he work at then? I mean, he must work

at something, his clothes look nice enough and he looks well-fed."

"He does a bit of this and a bit of that, Grandma."

"And what is *a bit of this and a bit of that*?" The gentle fishing was becoming an interrogation.

"I don't know, he never really said. I don't know him that well, Grandma, we're hardly old friends!" Florence tried to laugh it off, she could tell that her grandmother was suspicious, she just didn't know why. "He takes whatever work is available. I think that's a good thing, don't you? A young man who is willing to work hard and do whatever it takes to survive?"

"It depends what you mean by *whatever it takes*," Queenie said, and there was that strange steeliness in her eyes once again. "Well, I think I'm feeling a little better now, my sweet. And I've got work to do. That gin won't make itself now, will it?"

"Are you sure that you're all right?"

"I will be just fine, love," Queenie said and got herself up onto her feet with a smile.

The last ten minutes had been the strangest that

Florence could remember, and her grandmother's curious attitude towards Jimmy would be something that she wouldn't forget for a while, she was sure of it.

"I think I've made just about as much as I can carry to Newgate. It won't be much, but I'll sell all of it, no doubt about that," Queenie said and surveyed the bottles of gin lined up on the little wooden table.

"Are you sure, Grandma?" Florence said, doubting that Queenie, seeming to get frailer by the day, would manage that many bottles.

"Yes, I've managed to get the lend of a little wooden cart. A sort of trolley, I suppose. Well, a box with wheels on it." Queenie gave a hooting laugh.

"Won't you look a little bit suspicious outside Newgate prison wheeling a cart? Oh, Grandma, I don't want the peelers getting you."

"*Peelers?* My goodness, you're Limehouse through

and through now, aren't you?" Queenie was teasing her, but Florence was still concerned.

"I mean it, Grandma."

"You've never been to a public hanging, have you?" Queenie asked a rhetorical question for she already knew the answer to it.

"No," Florence said and shuddered at the very thought.

"There are people wheeling in all sorts of things for sale. It's as grand a day out as a county fair, believe me. They'll be jugglers, buskers, cake sellers, bread sellers, you name it. And I won't be the only one there selling a little drop of home-made gin either. It'll be a busy old affair, and the peelers will have enough on their plate without chasing an old woman with a wooden box on wheels."

"It just seems like an awful thing, Grandma," Florence said, but Queenie laughed.

"What, me selling gin, or some crook kicking his feet at the bottom of a rope?"

"Grandma!" Florence said, closing her eyes, her hand flying up to her mouth.

"That's the problem with you being raised over in Wimbledon. There's a hardness to life, for all of us. But that's *this* part of London for you. One man's downfall is another man's opportunity to put bread on the table for a week. I wish I could be as sensitive as you, my sweet, but I was raised in a place like this. I had a life where I couldn't afford to be sensitive. Public hangings are big events, opportunities that can't be missed, not by those of us who can't afford to miss them."

"I know," Florence said, but she didn't mean it. She hated the idea; it made her sick to her stomach. It reminded her that there was a hard side to Queenie, a brutally hard side, and she wished she never had to see it.

Florence knew that it was a hardness born of necessity, born of the same grinding poverty that she could see all around her in Limehouse. It didn't make it any easier for her to look at, however.

"And it's time to make the best of it because I've heard mutterings that they're going to put an end to public hangings. They'll be taking people off inside to do it soon, no spectators, no opportunity to make a few coins. There's always a do-gooder somewhere with a petition, isn't there?" Queenie said and her lips narrowed disapprovingly. *"It's 1867 and about time we were finished with this inhumane spectacle,"* she went on in a parody of the upper-class accent. "But those are the ones who can afford to bleat about humanity and dignity and all the other things they've been privileged enough to enjoy for a lifetime. Let them live as we do for a while, that's what I say. Let them try to survive in *our* London and see how long their humanity and dignity worries them then."

"I suppose so," Florence said without an ounce of commitment. She wanted to stop talking about this now. She'd never seen a public execution, but it didn't take a great deal of imagination to picture a human being hung by their neck, did it?

"Florence, it's just the way life is," Queenie said and clicked her tongue.

"I know, it just seems strange to spend Sunday morning sitting in a church and Sunday afternoon making gin so that our fellow churchgoers can enjoy something to drink whilst they watch a human being's life being taken away from them next week."

"I think it's time we talked about something else,

Florence. I shouldn't be this way with you, it isn't fair, you've been used to a better way of life."

"But didn't you get used to it too? All those years in Wimbledon, don't you miss it? Don't you think about it?"

"Of course, I think about it, child. I thought we were set for a lifetime there, really, I did. I was lucky to get that position with a baby granddaughter in my arms. I couldn't believe my luck when Mrs Daventry took me on."

"And I *was* a baby?" Florence said cautiously, remembering how Marcus had once told her she had been old enough to run around.

"Of course, you were a baby, Florence. What a strange question!"

"Did we go to Wimbledon straight after my mother died?"

"Yes, we did. I wanted something different for you, something better for you. I knew the streets of Whitechapel were no place to raise a child."

"So, we lived in Whitechapel?" Florence said, and Queenie looked flustered.

"For a time, yes."

"Had you always lived in Whitechapel, Grandma?"

"What's all this?" Queenie said with a huff and began to put cork stoppers into the gin bottles. "I feel like I'm being questioned by one of the peelers!"

"I just wondered what life was like before, that's all. You never talk about life before Wimbledon, that's all."

"Life before Wimbledon was very much like it is now, child. Grubby rooms like this, endless hours working in the mill like you do for next to nothing. Trying to find some way to put food on the table that doesn't see you up to your neck in trouble. That's what life was like. What's the point in talking about that?"

"You never talk about my mother," Florence went on, determined not to give up just yet.

"I suppose because you're so much like her, I forget sometimes that you're not her," Queenie said and sat down heavily on one of the wooden chairs, leaning her elbows on the table and resting her chin in her hands. "You look like her, especially now that you're getting a little older. Now that you've turned fourteen, there's hardly anything to tell between you and your mother when she was that age."

"And what else about her, Grandma? What was she like?"

"She was kind and sweet, like you. I suppose she wasn't quite as bright as you, not quite so sharp, but then she didn't have the benefit of learning to read and write the way you did in Wimbledon. I reckon reading and writing must change a person; it must open the world up to them a bit more."

"Only if you have books to read," Florence said wistfully, remembering the library at the house in Wimbledon and how the entire Daventry family had urged her to treat it as her own and help herself to any book she liked.

"She was sensitive like you," Queenie said and let out a great sigh, shaking her head from side to side.

"It sounds like you don't approve of sensitivity."

"It's not that I don't approve of it, my dear, it's just that I see how it leads people into danger. Sensitive people have bigger hearts and they let all manner of folk inside. It doesn't do to open your heart wide and let people in, Florence. If there is just one piece of advice that I can give you in this life, I daresay it would be that."

"Not to let people into my heart?" Florence said, and was once again reminded of the great differences between herself and her grandmother.

"You are never more vulnerable than when you do that. You are never more at risk, more in danger than when you openly trust somebody. Always remember, trust must be earned, and suspicions and niggling doubts must always be listened to."

"You make the world sound like a dreadful place, Grandma."

"The world isn't a dreadful place, Florence. *Our* London is a dreadful place. *Limehouse* is a dreadful place. What difference does the world make when all you can see are the miserable streets around you? When you live in the dark streets, in amongst the dirty buildings, you never see the rest of the world. There are folk here in Limehouse who've never left it, and that's the truth. There are folks here in Limehouse who would see Wimbledon with the same eyes that they might look at another country. You can only deal with what's around you, you can only live according to your own small world and that's it. So, I'll say again, don't leave your heart wide open for anybody to wander into it."

"I won't," Florence said, feeling her spirits plummet.

"Well, I suppose we'll see about that," Queenie said and pushed herself up from the table to set about her work once again.

CHAPTER SIX

*F*lorence's day at the mill had felt about forty feet long, never-ending, and backbreaking. After so many months of working there, she was beginning to feel the build-up of dust and lint in her airways. She imagined her lungs halfway full of the horrid thick fluff which choked the machines, the fluff which the smallest and most vulnerable amongst the workers had to climb in and pick out.

Once again, Florence was glad that her grandmother hadn't been taken on at the mill. That awful cough of hers seemed to get worse day after day, and the dust and heat of the mill room would have put Queenie into an early grave, Florence was sure of that.

Queenie had started to seem frail, and Florence could hardly think about it without tears filling her eyes. She knew her grandmother wasn't far from her sixtieth birthday, something of an achievement in a place like Limehouse. But Queenie had never seemed old, not before now. In Wimbledon, she had seemed vital and robust, even when she had started to slow a little and Florence had picked up the slack. She'd been ageing, but she'd been ageing well, with good food to fortify her and the fresh air of Wimbledon in her lungs.

The cough that plagued Queenie night and day now had, Florence was sure, begun in Wimbledon. However, it had deteriorated rapidly since they'd moved to Limehouse, and she couldn't help but think it was just one more reason to hate that awful place.

Florence was dragged out of her worrisome thoughts by the sight of Jimmy in the distance. She hadn't seen him for some days, and whilst he didn't always walk her from the mill to the door of the tenement, his absence this time had been rather lengthier. As the only bright spot on her horizon, Florence realised that she'd missed him.

She was still some distance from Jimmy, and it was

clear that he hadn't yet seen her. He was standing outside the Rose and Crown pub talking to two young women, *girls* really, probably not much older than Florence herself. She couldn't see them clearly from so far away, but they looked a little done up for so early in the evening. Still, it was autumn now and usually falling to a dusky darkness by the time Florence came out of the mill at the end of a very long day, and she couldn't see as clearly as she would have liked.

Florence continued to study the little scene with interest, seeing that one of the girls had bent her head and was looking down at the ground. She stayed that way for some moments and finally Jimmy reached out for her, laying his hands on her shoulders and stooping to peer into her face. It seemed like rather a tender gesture, and something about it made Florence feel a little jealous.

Deep down, Florence knew she didn't have a right to feel jealous. She knew that she still loved Marcus, that he would always be wedged firmly into heart, permanent, immovable. Whatever man came into her world, Florence would always compare him to that first love. Not just her *first* love, but her *only* love, she was so sure of it. She liked Jimmy, she was attracted to him, his handsome face and his bright ways. She cared for him a great deal, even though the extent of their friendship was the short walk from the textile mill to her front door in Limehouse. But she didn't love him; she could never love any man but Marcus.

Florence quickened her pace, still determined to get a better look at the girls Jimmy seemed so intent upon, despite her half-measure feelings for Jimmy. *Half-measure.* That made her smile to herself; that was the sort of thing that Queenie would have said.

Finally, Jimmy turned his head and saw her approaching. He quickly dispatched the two girls, tipping his head in the direction of the Rose and Crown. Without a word, the girls walked away from him and darted in through the door. Surely, they were a little young for such a place? Still, Florence didn't have much time to think about it, for Jimmy was now striding towards her with a wide and bright smile on his face.

"Is it that time again? The day has got away from me today, and that's the truth. I wanted to walk you all the way home, Florence Smith."

"You will have to save your money and get yourself a pocket watch, Jimmy," Florence said and laughed, her misgivings about the little scene she'd just witnessed already evaporating. There was something so disarming about Jimmy. Charming and disarming. Yes, that described him perfectly.

"Maybe I'll get myself one for my birthday."

"You know how to treat yourself!" Florence said, teasing.

"And you *don't* know how to treat yourself! You worked in that awful place on your birthday, didn't you?"

"Yes, I did." Florence shrugged, remembering that her fourteenth birthday some weeks before had hardly registered with her as she stood staring at the great long looms in the mill. "Everybody around here works on their birthday, don't they?" She couldn't help thinking about Wimbledon, about how Queenie had always made her a cake, how Marcus had always given her a little gift of some kind. And how Mr and Mrs Daventry had always wished her many happy returns.

"Not me! I always make sure I celebrate in style."

Jimmy was walking at her side now, and Florence felt the familiar reassurance of his tall and substantial physical presence.

"Do you now?" Florence asked with a laugh. "And just how do you celebrate in style?"

"I don't do a stitch of work all day, for a start. Then I have myself a little drop of gin and something nice to eat. It's only one day of the year, isn't it?"

"You drink gin?" Florence said, her surprised reaction immediately making her feel childish and unworldly. She just never imagined Jimmy drinking gin. Perhaps she had fallen into the ways of assuming he was just like Marcus. She was trying to replace Marcus with Jimmy, but they were two different people.

"This is Limehouse, Florence, everybody drinks gin. Everybody but you, by the looks of it," he said and started to laugh. As always, his laughter was light and friendly, there was no hint of cynicism or mocking. At least he never mocked her.

"I just don't like the taste," Florence said, her cheeks flushing a little at the lie; she had never taken so much as a teaspoon of gin her entire life.

"A fancy girl like you, champagne is probably more your tipple," he said, teasing her gently.

"Oh, not this again!" Florence laughed; she enjoyed this teasing.

"You should come down to the Rose and Crown tonight, Florence," he said, standing still for a moment, reaching out to touch her arm in a way which made her think of the girl he had just seemingly comforted.

"The Rose and Crown? I'm only fourteen, Jimmy, you forget that."

"Fourteen is a lot older here in Limehouse than it is over in Wimbledon, believe me. I know the landlord, he wouldn't turn you out if you walked in on my arm, sure as eggs is eggs."

"The landlord isn't the problem, Jimmy. Can you imagine what my Grandma would say?"

"I don't think she likes me very much," Jimmy said and winced.

"You've only met her once, and she wasn't feeling very well that day. You must have seen how pale she was," Florence said hurriedly, still feeling a little embarrassed about the way Queenie had glared at him with those steely grey eyes of hers. Even now, remembering the little scene made her feel awkward.

"I still don't think she likes me very much," Jimmy said and laughed. "And anyway, does she have to know where you're going? Can't you just say you're going out and that's that?"

"No, I can't. I've never done anything like that before, just setting off into the darkness. She just cares about me, that's all. She doesn't want me to get into any sort of trouble, to be in any sort of danger."

"I don't know whether to be insulted or pleased that you think you might be in some sort of danger with me," he said and gave her a slow, disturbingly attractive smile. "Maybe I should be pleased."

"I'm still new here to Limehouse, and yes, things really were different over in Wimbledon. I think she's worried I'm too soft for a place like this, she just wants to protect me. And I don't want to worry her, not while she's so unwell."

"What's wrong with her?" Jimmy asked, mercifully letting go of his idea of the two of them going to the Rose and Crown.

"She has this cough; it never seems to go. And I think it's painful, too, because sometimes she has to wrap her arms around her chest when she's coughing as if she needs to hold onto herself tightly."

"You'll be like that yourself if you keep working at that mill."

"I don't have any choice, Jimmy. I need the money, I need to work, and there isn't anything else out there. There's nowhere in Limehouse I could work in service, there just aren't those kinds of houses here."

"I reckon there must be better things to do than working in service or working in the mill."

"Like what?"

"Well, why don't you just let me have a good long think about that. I reckon there are easier ways to get by." Suddenly, he seemed to be as evasive as Queenie could be at times.

"Well? What job do you suggest?" Florence asked, pressing him.

"All in good time, Florence. All in good time." He laughed and then slowed his pace. "Your Grandma is on the doorstep again," he went on in a furtive voice. "I wonder if I should make myself scarce."

"No, don't do that, Jimmy. Just walk me up to the door as normal. If you dart away now, Grandma will think you have some reason to. Trust me, her bark is worse than her bite."

"I don't know, something tells me that you've got that upside down and back to front. She strikes me as the sort of woman whose bite is worse than her bark." Jimmy chuckled and Florence couldn't help but join him.

"It's getting cold to stand out on the doorstep, Grandma," Florence said as she and Jimmy walked up to the door.

"I was just worried about you, child," Queenie said, that steely look in her eyes again. "Well, time you were on your way, young man," she went on, turning to Jimmy, her manner so abrupt that Florence's face burned with embarrassment.

"Nicc to see you again, Mrs Smith," Jimmy said, somewhat sarcastically. "I'll see you, Florence," he went on and touched Florence's shoulder before turning to walk away.

Queenie's face turned ashen, and Florence couldn't help but think that Jimmy had only reached out to touch her in order to be antagonistic. Why couldn't they simply get on? They were the only two people in her world now, why couldn't they just be friends?

"I'll see you, Jimmy," Florence said quietly to his departing back before Queenie ushered her inside the tenement building.

"**G**randma, that was so rude. I wouldn't be surprised if Jimmy never spoke to me again after that!" Florence said, her anger refusing to be denied even as Queenie began to cough. "It's not like I have any other friends, is it? Or perhaps you don't want me to have a single friend in all the world! Perhaps you want me to be all alone and miserable with nothing in my world but the textile mill and this horrible room!"

"Florence!" Queenie said, gathering herself after her coughing fit. "This room might not be good enough for you, but it's all we can afford."

"I know, I know." Florence sat down at the table and

sighed loudly. "I just don't understand why you don't like Jimmy. You don't even know him."

"And you obviously don't know him either!" Queenie said, seeming both waspish and afraid all at once.

"All he does is walk me from the mill to this door, and even then, not every day. He's the only person in all of Limehouse who's had a kind word to say to me. Every day I stand in that mill and I can feel the daggers in my back. That Jenny is awful, and she's got them all against me. I don't care, I don't want to be friends with them, but it's exhausting. The only thing which makes the day bearable is the idea of a few minutes of happy conversation from that door to this one. Why would you want to take that away from me?"

"I just don't want you to see that boy again. It's for your own good, Florence."

"And just how is that for my own good? How do you know what's for my own good?"

"Because I'm older and wiser, Florence. That's all you need to know." Queenie was digging in her heels, becoming unbending, and it was a stance that

Florence recognised well. Queenie was going to win this argument; when she was in this mood, she always did.

"No, it's not all I need to know." Florence was nursing a little belligerence of her own.

"You are not to see that boy again. If he comes up to you in the street, you turn your head and you keep walking, do you hear me? You don't so much as say *hello* to him, do you understand?"

"No, I don't understand. I don't understand any of this, Gran." Florence could feel tears in her eyes; this was beginning to feel like an injustice.

"Just stay away from Jimmy Bates!" Queenie was getting red in the face.

"Bates? How do *you* know his name is Bates? That's more than I know about him!"

"You're still in my care, Florence Smith, and you'll do as I say. I forbid you to see that boy, and I expect you to do as you're told."

"No, I won't do as I'm told!" Florence said, banging her fist on the table in the purest frustration.

"Florence, you just don't know…" Queenie began and then started to cough so violently that she could hardly draw breath.

Unable to get enough breath in to sustain her, Queenie's lips turned a horrible purplish-blue shade. In a heartbeat, Florence forgot their argument. She was panicking, terrified, and so certain that her beloved grandmother was about to die.

"Grandma, Grandma," Florence said, getting up from the table and racing to Queenie who was leaning heavily on the back of a chair. "Just try to stay calm, just close your eyes and try to stay calm."

Queenie couldn't respond, but Florence saw her close her eyes, doing as she was told for once.

"Now slowly take in a breath, Grandma. Don't rush it, that's right…" Florence said, slowly drawing in her own breath, leading by example. She didn't want her grandmother, in her panic, to try to breathe in too quickly. If she did, it would just irritate her chest, it would make her cough again, and it would deny her the air she so desperately needed.

With her eyes still closed, Queenie Smith began to breathe in slowly and breathe out slowly. Florence watched as her grandmother's lips returned to their normal colour, that horrible bruised look becoming ordinary and rosy again. Holding on to Queenie's arm, Florence could feel that her grandmother's entire body was shaking.

"Come on, let's settle you down for a while." Florence allowed her grandmother to lean heavily on her as she took her across the room to the bed. "That's it, just lay down and relax. You've had a real turn this time."

"Thank you, my sweet," Queenie said with a trembling voice.

"Don't try to speak, just relax. Just give yourself some time to get over it."

"You're a good girl, Florence. I'm sorry I..." She was becoming breathless again.

"Don't speak, Grandma. It doesn't matter, none of it matters. All that matters is that you get better. It's all I want in the world. It's the only thing I want. I want you to get better, Grandma. I want you to get better," Florence said, and tears rolled down her cheeks.

She felt lightheaded herself; the whole experience

had been terrifying, and the relief which followed in the wake of it was almost as debilitating. She knew that, sooner or later, both the fear and the relief would be replaced with simple worry. Of course, the worry was anything but simple; it was an exhausting occupation, but one that Florence knew she could hardly avoid. Queenie was sick, very sick, and there was no denying it anymore. This wasn't just a little cough, a little something that she was having trouble shaking, this was serious.

Their argument now paled into insignificance, and Florence didn't have an ounce of spare capacity left with which to wonder why it was her grandmother seemed to despise Jimmy. It certainly wasn't a subject that she intended to raise with her again, not if this was the effect it was going to have on her. For now, all Florence could do was concentrate on Queenie's well-being. Everything else would have to wait.

CHAPTER SEVEN

Queenie braced herself against the wall as the coughing fit began. This time, it was over a little sooner, and she would have been relieved about it had she not taken her cotton handkerchief away from her mouth to find it spattered with blood. It wasn't the first time, but this was more blood than she'd coughed up before.

Florence talked endlessly of paying for a doctor to have a look at Queenie, but she knew there was no point to it. She knew something was growing there in her lung, something that didn't ought to be there, something that she was forever trying to shift to no avail. It was the very thing which had taken her own mother away from this world, and Queenie was realistic enough to know that there was no point throwing away good money on a doctor who would not, in the end, be able to save her.

All that mattered now was keeping hold of every penny she earned, letting those few coins build so that Florence would have something to keep her going when the end came for Queenie. But she had something more to do, something else to save her granddaughter from that went far beyond financial penury. She had to keep her away from Warren Bates' son. She had to keep her away from that boy, whatever it took.

It was getting dark outside and she knew that Florence would soon be home from the mill. Winter was coming, and Queenie was absolutely certain that she wouldn't survive it. It was time for action, while she could still do something to protect the granddaughter she loved more than life.

"Grandma," Florence said, dashing into the room with a gentle smile on that beautiful face of hers. "How are you feeling?"

"Not too bad, my sweet."

"Have you still been coughing a little less?" Florence asked with all the hope and expectation of youth. She was still so young; she could still hope for the best.

"A little, but I'm going out to see the doctor all the same." Queenie knew it was a lie, but how else would she get out of the house without Florence being suspicious?

"Now?" Florence asked, seeming pleased that her grandmother was finally going to get some help, but a little dismayed by the hour. "Could the doctor not have seen you earlier?"

"No, he's a busy man. I suppose that's a good sign," Queenie said and threw in her customary chuckle to make everything seem normal.

She knew, despite their dreadful row of so many weeks before, that Florence still walked along the street with Jimmy Bates. He didn't bring her all the way to the door anymore, but Queenie had made it her business to spy, even though she knew Florence would be so hurt by it. But she had to know, she had to see it with their own eyes. And she *had* seen it;

Florence was just the same as her mother. She was so willing to see the best in others that Queenie began to fear that Florence would be as blind to the likes of Jimmy Bates as Gladys had been. And where had it got Gladys? An early grave, that was where! If this was the last thing she did in her time on earth, Queenie was determined to put a stop to this friendship once and for all.

"Well, I'll walk with you, Gran," Florence said, wrapping her shawl around her shoulders again, making ready to go out.

"No, I can get myself there. And in any case, I need you to keep an eye on that stew dangling over the fire. I don't want it burning, and I don't want to take it off the heat now otherwise we won't be eating for hours. Just keep your eye on it, that's all I ask."

"It's getting dark outside," Florence said with concern.

"You forget that this is *my* London, child. You forget that I was raised in a place like this. I know how to go about, how to keep out of trouble, otherwise I wouldn't have made it this far, would I?" She was purposefully abrasive, even though her granddaughter's concern had touched her heart. But abrasive was what always made things seem right, normal. Anything other than her old self would make Florence suspicious.

"If you say so, Gran!" Florence said and laughed. "And I promise to keep my eye on the stew."

O nce she hit the cold night air, Queenie covered her mouth and nose with her shawl. There was something about the extreme cold which irritated her windpipe, and she didn't want to have a coughing fit before she'd managed to track that boy down.

With all the knowledge of her upbringing and her life lived outside of Wimbledon, Queenie made her way to the Rose and Crown. She'd done a little digging about Jimmy Bates, and she knew exactly what line of business he was in. If he was anywhere as the sun went down, it would be in or around that awful pub.

By the time she was in the general area, Queenie was already exhausted. Her slow and determined breathing was taking all her concentration, and everything she had planned to say to the young man had already drifted away from her, words and were ideas just out of her reach. When she saw him gently pushing a young girl towards an older man, Queenie already feared that she would act on pure emotion.

The girl wasn't much older than Florence, and by the time Queenie was close enough to see better, she could sce that she'd been crying. The old man stood with his hands in his pockets, sighing irritably, looking at Jimmy and shaking his head impatiently.

"We talked about this, Mavis. Once you've got this first one out of the way, it gets easier. You've got to start somewhere, haven't you? You don't want to end up in the workhouse, do you now?" His voice was gentle, wheedling and Queenie hated him right down to his bones. At that moment, she could have been listening to his father, there was nothing to choose between them. That wheedling tone, that pretence at care. She had to do whatever she could to save Florence from him, she couldn't lose another beloved girl.

Finally, the young girl took the older man's crooked

arm and walked away with him. Jimmy gave a sigh of relief, and then quietly chuckled to himself.

"I don't see what's so funny about what you just did, Jimmy Bates," Queenie said, standing behind him and momentarily enjoying the fact that she had startled him. He spun around and looked at her with some confusion.

"Mrs Smith?" he said, his voice so innocent and his tone so light that anyone but Queenie might have been fooled by it.

"Stay away from my granddaughter," she said in a low voice.

"Why should I? I haven't done anything to her!" Jimmy's tone was plaintive, even offended, and Queenie could have slapped his face for it.

"Not yet, but you will."

"What are you talking about? You don't even know me, old woman!" The mask finally slipped, and he gave her such a hateful stare that Queenie grinned. He was every bit the chameleon that his father had been. One moment charming and innocent, the next hateful.

"You're a chip off the old block, I make no mistake about that."

"What? You know nothing!" Jimmy took a step towards her, and Queenie wondered for a moment if he was about to strike her.

"Yes, a real chip off the old block! Going to hit me, are you? Just like that good for nothing father of yours!"

"No, I'm not going to hit you," Jimmy said, but it was clear that she had antagonised him to that point. Maybe it would be better if he did hit her. Maybe that would be the one thing which would turn Florence away from that boy for good. The one thing that would do it without her having to tell her the truth she had been hiding for so long. The truth she had been protecting her granddaughter from.

"You want to, I can see it in those dead, cold, pale eyes of yours. That's what gave you away, boy. That first day when I saw those eyes, I knew who you were. Only the devil had eyes like that, and since he swung from a rope twelve years ago, I knew you had to be his. I knew just who you were." Queenie was letting her emotion get away with her, she knew it, but try as she might, she just couldn't stop it.

"What?" His face dropped, and his entire body tensed. If ever Queenie had been in danger in her life, she had never been in more danger than she was now. "What do you know about my father?" His voice was a ragged whisper, Queenie had clearly shocked him to his core.

"Enough to know that you're following in his footsteps. A blind man could see that you were turning that young girl out to earn money for you in the worst way possible. I won't have that for Florence. I won't have that again."

"Again?" Jimmy said slowly, and Queenie realised that she'd made a great mistake; she could see realisation dawning in those disturbing pale blue eyes.

"I know your reputation, and I don't want you anywhere near my granddaughter." Queenie was trying to claw back the upper hand.

"No, no," Jimmy said and slowly shook his head from side to side. "That's not it. That's not it at all."

The shock was beginning to die down as a horrible, cruel cynicism overtook what should have been a handsome young face. He knew who she was now, there was no doubt about that. Queenie had acted on pure emotion, and she had given herself away.

"Just stay away from her. I don't want her being pushed towards an old man someday just like you pushed that poor young girl."

"But that's not all, is it? I see you, Queenie Smith. Or should I say, Queenie Goodyear?" All her fears were confirmed. "I'm right, aren't I? You're the old Crow who ran to the peelers and got my father hanged." There was something horribly menacing in his tone.

"I didn't get your father hanged, he got himself hanged." There was no point in trying to deny it. There was no point in pretending to be Queenie Smith any longer. "His own actions led him up the gallows steps, Jimmy, his own actions and nothing more. Do you really think he should have got away with what he did? Do you really want to follow in his footsteps? Because if you do, you'll be the one dancing at the end of a rope this time."

"You can dress it up however you like, old woman,

you and that daughter of yours got my father hanged. You took my father away from me; you! I don't care what you do what you say, you're the one who saw to it that I grew up without him."

"And it should have given you a chance to be a different man, shouldn't it? But it seems that rottenness runs through your veins. It's not his example, its blood."

"You should have kept your mouth shut, shouldn't you?" Jimmy took a step towards her, and Queenie drew in a breath that was so cold it made her cough. "And don't think I care anything for an old bat like you coughing her guts up. You can cough yourself to death for all I care, I'm not going to help you," Jimmy said, and let out a cruel, hard laugh.

Queenie staggered sideways, leaning against one of the ornate lampposts that made Limehouse somehow look more grubby for all their neatness. She couldn't speak, she couldn't stop coughing. She could taste the blood in her mouth; her eyes closed and her ears filled with that horrible laughter.

"You took my father from me, and I'm going to make you sorry for that, old woman." And with that, he walked away from her. He left Queenie, old and frail, clinging to a lamppost and coughing up blood. He really was a chip off the old block. As she finally began to gather herself, Queenie knew that she had made everything so much worse.

CHAPTER EIGHT

Florence had been worried about Queenie for days, and she was itching for her shift at the mill to finish so that she could go back to their room in the tenement and check on her.

Queenie had seemed a little better, physically, but something was troubling her and Florence, try as she might, couldn't get to the bottom of it. She'd wondered if it had something to do with the doctor if he'd told Queenie some sort of awful bad news that Queenie was now keeping to herself. But Florence had questioned her over and over again about the doctor, and Queenie had simply shrugged it off, telling Florence that he'd assured her it was just a little cough and that she would shake it off soon.

"You'd better concentrate, or you won't be Mr Mason's pet anymore, Flo." Jenny just couldn't help herself; try as she might, she couldn't get from one end of the day to the other without saying something spiteful.

"I've never been Mr Mason's pet, and it's Florence, not Flo," Florence said, not even bothering to turn and look at the girl. It was already dark outside, and surely the time for going home couldn't be far away. There was no sense in ruining her evening by entertaining an argument with a pathetic girl who was truly no more than a simple irritation to her.

"Flo, Flo, Flo," Jenny was singing under her breath.

"Just shut up!" Florence hissed her voice filled with menace, and Jenny was surprised enough to do just that.

The end of the working day couldn't have come soon enough, not just so that she might get away from the annoying Jenny, but so that she could hasten home and check on her grandmother. She tied her thick shawl around her shoulders, pulling the heavy woollen fabric close around her ears to guard against the cold, and set off into the darkness.

Florence smiled when she saw the familiar outline of Jimmy just a few yards away, standing with his back to her. She hadn't seen him for a couple of days, and she realised that she was pleased, once more, that he had returned. She felt a little guilty these last weeks, defying her grandmother and continuing her friendship with the handsome young man, but she needed a little something in her life. She needed that friendship otherwise all that would be left would be the mill and her worries.

"Long time no see, Jimmy," Florence said lightly, running up behind him.

However, Jimmy turned sharply, and for a moment she wondered if she had made a mistake. There was something in his face which made him look so different that she could almost have been convinced that it was another young man altogether. Those pale blue eyes were narrowed to slits, and the familiar smile was noticeable by its absence. His lips were pressed together at first, creeping sideways into a snarl of sorts as he glared at her.

"Jimmy? What's the matter?"

"Like you don't know, Florence!" he said, hardly

moving as he stood as still as a statue, his face just a few inches from hers. Something about the change in him made her feel suddenly afraid, Florence backed away a little by instinct. However, Jimmy reached out and seized her wrist hard, stopping her going anywhere.

"Jimmy, stop that! Let me go now, Jimmy Bates!" Florence said, tears in her eyes as hurt and confusion almost overwhelmed her. "Just let me go."

"I will not let you go, Florence Smith! Or should I say, Florence Goodyear?" He said and started to laugh. It wasn't the laugh she was used to; it wasn't the light, pleasant laugh. It was something much crueller, much harder.

"Goodyear? What are you talking about?" Florence said, the first tear rolling down her cheek as she twisted her arm this way and that in an attempt to free herself.

"You don't need to keep pretending!" he said, holding her all the tighter the more she struggled. "All these months, you must have been laughing up your sleeve at me! That little head of yours held high, thinking you're so much better than everybody else when you're nothing of the sort!"

"Jimmy, I don't know what you're talking about. I don't know why you're calling me Goodyear when my name is Smith." She stopped struggling, and Jimmy suddenly released her arm. She immediately rubbed her already bruised wrist with her other hand.

"You don't *know*, do you?" Jimmy said slowly as if he was just realising something. The sneer began to creep across his face again, only this time there was a little pleasure in it. It was still angry, about what she did not know, but he was also a little triumphant now.

"Know what? What are you talking about?" Florence pulled a handkerchief from the pocket of her skirt and hastily rubbed at her face, angry with herself for being reduced to tears when she should be standing up for herself. But it had all come as such a shock; she thought Jimmy was her friend, that he cared about her.

"You really don't know, do you?"

"I suppose not," Florence said and shrugged. "Look, I

don't know what's the matter with you today, but I don't want to walk home with you. I want to go by myself," Florence made to walk around him, but Jimmy reached out and seized her arm again, only this time a little less harshly.

"Oh no you don't, not until I've given you your history, Florence Goodyear."

"Smith. It's Florence Smith."

"No, it's Florence Goodyear. Daughter of Gladys Goodyear, the little tart who got my father hanged."

"Hanged? Your father?" Florence's mouth fell open. "You didn't tell me your father was hanged."

"I'm surprised that old hag of a grandmother didn't tell you. She is as much to blame as that daughter of hers."

"My mother is dead, Jimmy. She died giving birth to me, I told you that before."

"No, she didn't die giving birth to you," he said and started to laugh. "Although she probably wished that she did. She'd never have been able to fix a father's name to you, after all. I mean, she wouldn't have known who it was, would she? What with so many..." Before he had a chance to finish, Florence slapped him hard around the face.

She had slapped him before she had even thought about doing such a thing, it was a reflex, an instinct, her heart acting without giving her head a moment's notice. For a split second, she felt afraid; would he retaliate? After all, it would seem that she didn't know Jimmy Bates as well as she thought she did.

"What an awful thing to say! You don't know my mother, how dare you?" Focusing fully on his words, Florence let go of her fear and allowed her anger to take over. "I don't know what's wrong with you, Jimmy, but I don't care to stand here trying to find out. You horrible, horrible boy!"

"I'm not a boy, Florence Goodyear, I'm a man. A young man, like my father was when your mother got him hanged."

"Not that again!"

"It looks like that grandmother of yours has really kept you in the dark, doesn't it? Maybe you should go home and ask her to tell you all about her wonderful daughter Gladys, the prostitute." He threw his head back and laughed, distracting himself well enough that Florence was able to yank her arm away from his grip. She backed away from him and was relieved to note that this time, he didn't pursue her.

"That's an awful thing to say. You rotten, awful liar, Jimmy Bates. My Grandma must have seen something in you that I was too foolish to see. No wonder she told me I couldn't see you anymore! I only wish I'd listened to her. She must have seen your spiteful ways in your eyes. I reckon I'd do better to listen to her in the future."

"Listen to someone who's been lying to you since you with this high?" He said and reached down to indicate the height of a small child. "I'm not sure somebody like that is worth listening to."

"You just stay away from me in future. I don't want to hear any more of your lies, any more of your ugly stories, and I don't want to see your face again." Giving him a wide berth, Florence darted around him and began to run for home.

"That's right, you run as fast as you can, Florence Goodyear. You run home and ask Queenie Goodyear why she changed your name. Why she changed her own name. And use your brain, girl!"

He called out after her, causing a group of small children to stare openly. "Work out why it is you and your grandmother have the same surname! If you had a father, he'd have given you his name. I know what you are!"

This, above all things, struck a nerve. Smith or Goodyear, Florence had often wondered why it was she had the same surname as her maternal grandmother. She'd always suspected that her mother and father had never married. Queenie being Queenie, Florence had never liked to ask her, and so she had chosen to assume that her mother had simply married a man whose name was also Smith. After all, Smith was just about the most common name in all of England. But Goodyear? That wasn't quite so common, was it?

Florence shook her head and kept running. It didn't matter if Goodyear was a common name or not, it wasn't her name. For reasons of his own, Jimmy Bates was lying. Perhaps he just wanted to hurt Queenie, knowing that the woman just didn't like him. And in not liking him, it turned out that Queenie was right all along; she was just older and wiser.

"What's the matter with you, my sweet?" Queenie said as Florence hurried into the room, her face stained with tears despite her attempts to clean herself up. "Have you been running? Your breathing sounds worse than mine!"

"I'm all right, Grandma," Florence said, hardly knowing where to begin and, worse still, hardly knowing if she ought to begin. Suddenly she felt as if her feet were on very unsteady ground, and she didn't dare take a step for fear of falling into a world she didn't know existed.

"No, you're not," Queenie said and pulled out one of the chairs at the little wooden table. "Sit."

"I'm all right, I promise." Florence sat down at the table, turning her face slightly away from Queenie.

"You been crying, and you've been running. What happened?" Queenie's own breathing began to pick up speed, and Florence was horribly aware of doing or saying anything that would precipitate an awful attack of coughing. "Was it him? Was it Jimmy Bates?"

"How did you know?" Florence said, wishing that she knew the truth of everything. "How did you know he was such an awful person?"

"I just did."

"But why didn't I see it?"

"Has he touched you? Has he done something to you?" Queenie's lips began to go thin with anger.

"No, it isn't what he did," Florence said, deciding not to tell Queenie that he had gripped her arm so painfully. "It's what he said."

"Said?" Queenie said, and Florence thought she saw a flicker of fear in her eyes. What was going on? What did all this mean?

"He said the most awful things. He said that my name is really Florence Goodyear, and he said that my mother did something to have his father hanged. I didn't even know his father had been hanged," Florence said and shrugged, but there was a look in her grandmother's eyes now which stopped her in her tracks.

"You really shouldn't take any notice of..."

"It's true, isn't it?" Florence said, almost pinning her grandmother to her seat with a most determined stare. Florence refused to look away, and she could see Queenie's expression changing moment by moment. She looked cornered, like a fox before the hounds.

"It's just a name, my sweet."

"So, I *am* Florence Goodyear. And you *are* Queenie Goodyear." Florence's heart was beating like a drum, and still, she stared at her grandmother. "*Both* of us Goodyear, isn't that strange?"

"So, your mother wasn't married to your father. For heaven's sake, Florence, that's life in a place like this. Your mother didn't have the privilege of growing up in a nice house in Wimbledon."

"You're not going to put me off that way, Grandma. I've always known that there were things you weren't telling me, things that you were hiding. For one thing, I wasn't a baby, a tiny baby, when we first went to Wimbledon, was I?"

"No, you weren't."

"And my mother didn't die giving birth to me, did she?"

"No, she didn't. You weren't quite two, I suppose, when she died."

"Why didn't you tell me?" Florence asked, tears rolling down her face. "Why did you keep so much from me? She was my mother, why didn't you tell me she lived long enough to hold me and to know me, and to love me?"

"Please don't be angry with me, Florence. If you knew the truth of it all, you'd know why I went to such great lengths to protect you."

"I want the truth of it all, Gran. I want to hear every bit of it."

"It was all such a long time ago."

"No, that won't do. I've just had Jimmy Bates shouting in my face; how can you protect me from that? And how can I protect myself, defend myself, unless I know the truth?"

"I thought we'd be completely unknown here. I know it's not far from Whitechapel, but why, oh why, did Warren Bates' boy have to come here to Limehouse?

He should have stayed in Whitechapel like that good for nothing father before him." Queenie let out a great sigh and leaned heavily against the table.

"How did my mother get Warren Bates hanged?"

"She didn't. Warren Bates got himself hanged."

"For what?"

"For murder." Queenie began to blink furiously, and Florence realised that her grandmother was fighting back tears, something she never ordinarily had to do.

"Who did he murder?" Florence said, her mouth going dry.

"My daughter. Your mother."

"Oh, no," Florence said, and the tears flowed freely down her face. She had no memory of her mother whatsoever, and yet the news that her mother had been murdered affected her dreadfully, tearing at her heart and making her feel hot and sick.

"I just didn't want you to know it. I didn't want you to be as hurt as you are now."

"And you didn't want me to know that she was a prostitute," Florence said, and finally the tears rolled down Queenie's face too. "It's true, isn't it? What Jimmy Bates said, it really is true."

"I was married late and widowed early. I was passed twenty-eight years old when I had my Gladys. I'd never much caught anybody's eye before Maurice Goodyear came along. He was a little bit older, but he was a good man. Oh, and I loved him. I loved him so much that I felt like a young girl again. When Gladys came along, my world was complete. I had the man I loved, and I had this beautiful little girl all of my own to take care of. It was everything I'd ever wanted, Florence," Queenie said, not bothering to dry her tears. Her voice was gentler now, not its usual harsh, abrupt tone.

"Oh, Grandma," Florence said, reaching out to take Queenie's hand.

"And then, when Gladys was just fourteen, Maurice died. He just up and died, I never did know what had caused it. Suddenly, there we were, mother and daughter without a penny to our names. He'd worked hard, my Maurice, but there was never anything spare to put by for a rainy day. We had nothing."

"What happened?"

"I went out to work, travelling every day over to that factory making matches. Came home every night stinking of phosphorus, terrified that something would have happened to my Gladys whilst I was out."

"She was fourteen, Grandma. Surely she would have been all right."

"No, she was too much like her father. Too trusting, too willing to give people the benefit of the doubt. I'd worried about her for her whole life, always trying to make her a little bit harder, a little bit tougher, but failing. Oh, but she was a kind girl. She wanted to make things easier, to go out and find a little work of her own. Unfortunately, there was no textile mill here at the time, and there wasn't a place for her at the match factory. She told me that she got herself a little job in the Dog and Duck, a pub just two streets away from where we lived. She was helping out the landlord, washing pots, that type of thing," Queenie said and shook her head sadly.

"But she wasn't?"

"No, she wasn't. Before she was fifteen, she was

already under the spell of Warren Bates. That man." Queenie shook her head again. "That rotten, evil man."

"What was he like? What did he do?"

"He was the one that turned her into a prostitute. So yes, it is true, my beloved daughter, my only child, worked as a prostitute to help keep a roof over both our heads. I'll never forgive myself for it, and I'll never forgive myself for not realising it until it was all too late."

"But if she didn't tell you, how were you to know?" Florence felt utterly heartbroken, but she had to hear the rest. She had to know all of it.

"She was my child; I should have known it by instinct. I was so tired, Florence. I was so tired of working six full days a week in that awful place, working my guts out on a Sunday to keep the awful little room we lived in clean."

"How did you find out?"

"When I finally realised that she was expecting a child. She was just seventeen years old, and it broke my heart. I tore into her as if she wasn't even my daughter, and I'll never forgive myself for that either. In the end, when I asked her again and again to tell me the name of the father, she told me that she didn't know. She'd had enough of me shouting and yelling at her, you see, and finally, the truth came out. She had been working, and the money she'd been giving me to help keep us going has been earned by prostitution. She'd never thrown anything in my face before, but she did that night. And even now, all these years later, I don't blame her. If I'd been a better mother, she might have been able to come to me sooner."

"What about this Warren Bates? You said she had fallen under his spell."

"He was older than her, four or five years, and every bit as handsome as that boy of his. He was like the Pied Piper to my Gladys, he only had to whistle his tune and she would run to him. The times I tried to tell her that if he truly loved her, he would never have sent her out like that, off with other men. What man could really bear the love of his life laying down with different men night after night?" Queenie stared vacantly into the middle distance and shook her head, whilst Florence felt more and more nauseous.

"But she wouldn't listen to you?"

"No, she wouldn't listen to me. We never fought, not until him. And he was the only thing we ever did fight about. She was so naive, so gentle, just like a father had been. Too gentle for this world and the hateful men in it. The likes of Warren Bates who can see a timid girl a mile off and work his magic on her."

"He didn't love her, then?"

"No, he didn't love anybody. Worse still, he already had a wife of his own. But Gladys was mesmerised by him."

"He wasn't my father, was he?" Florence asked, suddenly dismayed to think that Jimmy might be her brother, especially after the way he had just treated her.

"No, he wasn't. As much as she loved him and followed him around everywhere, he didn't put his hands on my Gladys until after you'd been born."

"But why? Why then?"

"Because she was young and beautiful, and he needed the money that could make for him. You see, when you were born, I convinced her to stop. She stayed home with me, and she looked after you so well. She was such a kind and caring girl, a natural mother in ways that I've never been. She loved you so much, Florence. And she always called you Florence. Never Florrie, never Flo, always, always Florence," Queenie said and smiled sadly at the memory. "But she never did know who your father was. I suppose I didn't want you to know that, or any of it."

"My poor mother," Florence said sadly, and her eyes began to fill with tears again. "But what happened to her?" Florence blew her nose loudly. "I mean, why did Warren Bates murder her?"

"She was just nineteen years old, and you only just starting to walk. She'd been back to him so many times, just for a week or two here and there, but she always came home, each time learning a little bit more about that man and his character. In the end, the spell was broken, and she decided once and for all to let go of that life, to stay home with me and concentrate on you."

"What happened?"

"He kept trying to get her to go back to him, and so she decided to go out and tell him properly. I think there was a part of her that still loved him, and that gentle side of her truly thought she owed him a proper explanation, even after everything he'd made her do. So, she went to meet him. He kept a room upstairs in the Dog and Duck, away from his wife and child. He ran his business from there, with the permission of the landlord, of course. Anyway, I can only assume that she told him she was done with it all, that she didn't want him, and she didn't want that life."

"And that's when he murdered her?"

"He strangled the life out of her. She'd been gone for hours, and I just knew in my heart that something was wrong. I took you to an elderly lady who lived a few doors away and I went to the Dog and Duck. I got in past the landlord and darted up the stairs, and I burst into his room. And there she was, my little girl, laying on the floor, her lips blue, her face bruised, and that foul pig's finger marks on her neck. He was in there too; he was so shocked to see me. I started to scream, I started to attack him, and that's when the landlord came up the stairs. He took one look at my Gladys and almost passed out. I knew I had to go for the police, I had to tell somebody. I couldn't let that man get away with what he'd done to my little girl." Queenie began to cry in earnest, her sobs enough to break Florence's heart in two.

"Grandma, I'm so sorry. I'm so, so sorry." Florence realised then just how awful it must have been for Queenie to see her with Jimmy Bates, a young man who looked so much like the father who had taken her only child from her.

"And I'm sorry I didn't tell you. I wanted to be away from it all, all the talk, just being in Whitechapel, seeing the same old faces, the same old streets, everything reminding me of everything I'd lost. First Maurice, and then my Gladys. All I had left in the world was you, that precious little girl who was so innocent. I suppose I didn't want to risk it. I wanted to get you away from there, to find something different. The Lord knows where I found the courage and the confidence to do it, I suppose I must have been motivated by the purest grief."

"And so, you went to Wimbledon?"

"I went to Wimbledon. Mind you, I didn't know I was in Wimbledon until somebody told me. I just walked and walked with my bag of things and you in my arms and I kept going until I saw nicer houses. Not the poshest of the posh, just good houses that might possibly take me on. I was looking for folk who couldn't afford the best of servants, but still needed servants. And I suppose it helped that I said I was willing to work for nothing more than the roof over my head."

"Oh Gran," Florence said.

"Not that Mr Daventry took me up on that offer. They always paid me; I'll give them their due. It wasn't much, but they always paid me. And I had a roof over my head and a nice place to live. They never realised quite what it meant to me to get work there. I always felt like they'd helped me to save you, even though they had no idea of it."

"Thank you, Grandma. Thank you for going to such lengths for me. I'm not angry with you for not telling me everything, I love you so much. You did everything you could to keep me safe, and I'll never, ever forget that."

"I just wish that things had been different, that my Gladys might have lived and that you might have grown up knowing your mother. I'd have stayed right there in Whitechapel for the rest of my days just to have my Gladys alive again. But it wasn't to be, it was never meant to be."

"And Warren Bates was hanged for my mother's murder?"

"He was. It was the first time I'd ever seen a public execution, but the devil himself couldn't have kept me away that day. And he knew I was there," Queenie said and nodded. "Before they put that hessian sack over his head, he looked over at me. And you know what I did? I smiled. May God forgive me I smiled at him. I was going to watch him die and I was there to gloat, and I wanted him to know it. I bought three swigs of gin from an old lady selling the stuff she'd made at her kitchen table, and I thoroughly enjoyed myself. Right up until I saw that little boy." Queenie bowed her head.

"Little boy?" Florence said with some confusion. "Oh, you mean Jimmy?"

"He was only little, five or six, but he knew what was happening. He was sobbing his heart out, standing there holding his mother's hand. And that wife of his, what a wretch. She was so bedraggled, so downtrodden, that my heart went out to her. How she found the strength to go there on that day and support the man who had treated her so badly, I'll never know. Perhaps she did it for the child. Perhaps she wanted Warren Bates to know, in the end, that his little boy was right there with him."

"Oh, that's awful. But what could you have done about it? It wasn't your fault, Grandma. Warren Bates had killed my mother. Jimmy might think that his father was snatched from him, but what about my mother? She was snatched from me, and at the hands of his father. I feel sorry for the little boy he was, but I feel sorrier for you and for my mother. You were as innocent in all of this as he was."

"I'll never forget his little face. But he's changed, Florence. Just you remember that he's not a little boy anymore, he's a grown man. He's a grown man who can change like that," Queenie said and leaned across the table to snap her fingers just an inch or so from Florence's ear. "Don't you ever, ever trust him. He's full of charm, just like his father was, a real chameleon. He'll smile one minute and stick a knife between your ribs the next. If ever I saw a chip off the old block, it's that young man. That lack of feeling for others, that wasn't learned by him, he was too little to have learned it. It's in his blood, it's in his bone marrow. It's who he is, just like it was who Warren Bates was. Promise me you'll never be taken in by him."

"After the way he spoke to me tonight, Grandma, I think I can safely promise you that I'll be having nothing more to do with Jimmy Bates. I don't blame him for what his father did, but I do blame him for everything he said.

"I'm sorry for everything I've have had to tell you, Florence, but I'm glad it's finally out. It seems strange, but it's a relief. It's a relief that we don't have any secrets anymore."

"And nobody, not even Jimmy Bates, can hold it over your head now. I know everything, and he can't hurt us. We've got each other, Grandma, and that's all that counts."

"That's my girl," Florence said and leaned across the table to kiss the top Florence's head.

Florence realised that, as devastated as she was to hear the truth, she was relieved too. She'd always known that there was something to tell, she'd always suspected that it was something painful, and it had always been there like a monkey on her back. But that was gone now, and she felt she knew and understood her mother a little more than she had done at the beginning of the day. She closed her eyes and made a silent promise to her mother in heaven that she would never, ever make the same mistakes.

CHAPTER NINE

"Grandma, you look done in. I wish you wouldn't go to the public hangings. I don't think it does you any good." Florence took the small wooden box with wheels from Queenie. Without its aid to balance, Queenie almost toppled over.

"Wait, I just need to lean on it a minute," Queenie said, gripping the wooden handle and steadying herself.

"It's not safe, it's got wheels. Here, take my arm, let me get you over to the bed." No sooner had Florence helped her grandmother to sit down than Queenie suffered a terrible coughing fit. Unable to get her handkerchief to her mouth in time, she coughed blood all down the front of the old dress she was wearing.

Florence cried out in dismay. "Oh, no!" Florence was shaking from head to foot. "I'll run for the doctor."

"There's no need, there really is no need," Queenie wheezed, gripping Florence's wrist hard.

"But that's blood," Florence objected, feeling sick with shock.

"It's not the first time and I'm sure it won't be the last." Queenie had steadied her breathing surprisingly well, and she seemed intent on calming Florence down. "It just looks worse because I wasn't able to get my handkerchief up in time. Now calm down, my sweet, and see if we've got any tea leaves left. I could quite fancy a nice hot cup of tea. That will put me to rights, you see if it doesn't."

Reluctantly, Florence did as her grandmother asked. She filled a little pan with some water and hung it on the hook over the fire. Water boiled quickly over the fire, and so she quickly spooned just a few tea leaves into the old chipped teapot that Queenie had managed to buy from the flea market.

She kept her eye on Queenie the whole time, seeing how her body juddered now and again as she tried to hold back the coughing. Florence knew it was for her benefit, and it was breaking her heart. Her grandmother was very, very sick, and yet she was trying to act as if nothing was happening, nothing out of the ordinary.

"Once you've drunk your tea, I think you should lay down for a while, Gran. And I really do think that it's time for you to speak to the doctor. I know you didn't speak to him the last time you said you were going to."

"I'm sorry I lied to you, child, but I wanted to get out there and find that Jimmy Bates. I wanted to keep him away from you, although I can see now that I should have just told you the truth and that would have done the job a lot better."

"Never mind Bates now, he's not important. You're important, and I want a doctor to look at you."

"And you're important to me, Florence, and if anything happens to me, I want there to be some money left for you to rely on. As far as I see it, it's either a cough I will get over and to see a doctor would be to waste money, or it's a cough that I will never get over, something no doctor can do anything about, and so to see him would, again, be a waste of money. I don't like doctors, Florence, you know that."

"And it might be something serious that will get better if you see a doctor. Grandma, you're always so awkward."

"I know, I've always been a little bit awkward," Queenie chuckled and then coughed, only this time she had her handkerchief at the ready and she stowed it away in her pocket as soon as she'd finished using it so that Florence couldn't see the blood.

"Please let me fetch him," Florence begged.

"We'll see, for now, I don't feel any worse than I normally do, so let's hold onto the money for the time being. I'm even going to do exactly as you tell me. Look, I'm going to lay down and have a little sleep." Queenie gave her granddaughter a mischievous grin.

Florence wasn't fooled. She wasn't a child anymore; she was a young woman of fourteen with enough worries on her shoulders to qualify her as an adult. And she knew, without a doubt, that Queenie was playing her like a fiddle. She was awkward and obstinate, and even in sickness would undoubtedly be determined to have her own way. Well, if things got even an inch worse, Florence was already determined that Queenie wouldn't have her way any longer. If Florence had to march out of that room and fetch the doctor back herself, she would do just that, and no amount of complaining from her grandmother would change it. Queenie had always looked after her, *ferociously*, and now it was time for Florence to return the favour.

Queenie had such a disturbed night that Florence didn't sleep a wink. Her grandmother had definitely taken a turn for the worst, and she knew that she would run out for the doctor as soon as the sun came up over London.

Leaving Queenie in a fitful sleep, Florence washed and dressed and wrapped her heavy shawl around her shoulders. She hurried through the Limehouse streets, her breath forming white, swirling whisks on the cold early winter air. It was Saturday morning, and she should already have been at the mill. But how could she leave Queenie alone?

Seeing that the doctor's office was still closed, Florence realised that it was probably too early for him to be up and about his business. With that in mind, she quickened her pace and made her way to the mill. She had no intention of working that day, but she would do what she could to smooth things over with Mr Mason.

Hurrying in through the doors, she could feel as well as hear the awful noise coming from the mill room. She peered through the glass in the door to the mill room looking for any sign of Mr Mason. Jenny was standing alone, her face a perpetual scowl, no doubt silently complaining to herself about Florence's failure to turn up. For once, Jenny was going to have to put in a full day's work, no slacking, no waiting for Florence to take the lion's share.

Florence turned away from the mill room and scurried along to the offices. She'd only been in Mr Mason's office once, and as she approached the door, her quaking stomach was a very good indication of the fear she felt. She knocked on the door, pushing it open gently when Mr Mason bellowed that she should enter.

"Where have you been? You should have been here half an hour ago!" he barked like an angry dog.

"Mr Mason, I really am so sorry, but my Grandma has taken a horrible turn in the night. She's been coughing up blood, and there isn't anybody else to look after her. I just ran to the doctor's office, but he's not in there yet."

"Are you trying to tell me that you won't be working today, girl?" Mr Mason said giving no hint that the awful story she had just told him had any effect whatsoever.

"It just isn't possible, Mr Mason. It was hard enough to leave her to run for the doctor. She really is very sick; I wouldn't stay away from work for anything less."

"Well, I suppose time will tell about that," he said cynically. "Well, you won't be paid for the day, obviously. And I expect to see you here bright and early on Monday morning, otherwise, you will be looking elsewhere for a job."

"Thank you, Mr Mason," Florence said, having to force out her thanks to a man who had neither grace nor compassion. As Queenie would have said, he was Limehouse through and through.

"Well, no sense in you hovering here. Go on, on

your way."

With a small sense of relief, Florence hurried away from the mill and back to the doctor's office. With a greater sense of relief, she could see him inside and dashed in to plead with him to make a house call on Queenie. He agreed and said that he would be along in half an hour.

Florence was breathless by the time she returned to their room, leaving the door a little ajar so that the doctor when he arrived, would quickly work out which of the tenement's doors he was aiming for.

"What are you doing back from work?" Queenie asked, her voice a little far-off, her eyes barely open.

"Mr Mason has let me have a day away from the mill. That gives me all of today and all of Sunday to help you get better, Grandma," Florence said gently, taking the cloth from the bowl of cold water by the bed and wringing it out gently before applying it to Queenie's forehead. "You're very warm, Gran."

"I don't feel very warm. I feel frozen to the bone. Could you light a fire, my sweet?"

"The fire is already lit," Florence said, a little

dismayed that Queenie hadn't even realised it. "But I'll put a little extra wood on, see if that warms you up a bit."

"Thank you," Queenie said in an exhausted voice.

As Florence set about building up the fire, she was startled by a rather loud knock on the door. She turned in time to see the doctor already making his way in. He seemed a pleasant enough man, if a little aloof and brusque, and Florence was pleased that he didn't waste any time staring around at their meagre possessions and ragged accommodations.

"Mrs Smith, I'm Dr Peters." He surprised Florence by sitting down on the edge of the bed.

"Good morning, Dr Peters," Queenie said, and Florence had a terrible sense of doom. She had expected her grandmother to argue, to be obstinate, but instead, she simply looked grateful to see him. Surely, she was even sicker than Florence had thought.

Florence hovered, and as Queenie turned her head, it was clear that her pillow was horribly bloodstained. The doctor seemed to take it in his stride and asked Queenie if she was able to sit up so that he might have a listen to her chest with his stethoscope.

Between them, the doctor and Florence sat Queenie up, and after another coughing fit and a good deal of blood, the doctor was finally able to listen to her chest. Once Queenie was set back down on the bed, the doctor began to go through his bag. Florence hovered at a distance, not wanting to miss anything if he gave Queenie any information at all.

"Mrs Smith, I do believe you're in some pain, aren't you?" he asked gently.

"A little, doctor," Queenie said, her eyes turned away as if this was some dreadful, shameful admission. For a woman who had been as strong as an oak tree her entire life, perhaps that was exactly how it felt.

"A lot, I think," he said and gave Queenie a conspiratorial smile. Queenie didn't respond, she just nodded. "I'm going to leave some powders here for you, Mrs Smith. Your granddaughter can mix a teaspoon with some water whenever you have the pain in your lungs. It should make you comfortable, even allow you to sleep a little."

"Thank you, doctor," Queenie said, and her eyes

drifted closed. She was almost instantly asleep.

Dr Peters took off his stethoscope and put it back in his bag, leaving the bag on the floor before making his way across the room to Florence. His face looked grave, almost apologetic, and she braced herself for the worst.

"I can be quite sure that there is a devastating growth in your grandmother's left lung. Her breathing is such that I suspect it has grown out of all proportion, and I'm afraid that it is only a matter of time before she succumbs to it."

"But can't something be done to get rid of the growth?" Florence asked, her entire being already fighting against the diagnosis.

"It is a tumour, my dear, and it is very much a part of the lung now. There was a stage at which it might have been removed by surgery, but I'm afraid to say that such surgery is rarely successful. I really am very sorry, Miss Smith, and I am afraid that the very best I can do is leave you with these powders to make her last days more comfortable."

"Days?" Florence said, almost sinking to her knees. "Do you mean she only has days to live?"

"I'm so sorry," the doctor said, reaching out to take Florence's elbow, steadying her. "I'm afraid there really is nothing more I can do for her. To tell you to come and fetch me if you need me would be to take money off you that I'm sure you cannot spare. And it would be without a point because your grandmother cannot be cured."

"I see," Florence said, everything seemed unreal, even her own voice. "Well, thank you for the powders, and thank you for coming out to see her. How much do I owe you?"

"Nothing, my dear. I have done little enough, and I do not need to take money that you will undoubtedly need for the sake of a few minutes out of my day."

"I don't think my Grandma would like that, sir. She always pays her debts," Florence said, tears streaming down her face.

"Then perhaps it should be our little secret," the doctor said with a kindly smile as he tapped the edge of his nose. "Take care of yourself. These next days will not be easy ones for you."

"Thank you. You've been very kind," Florence said, and as the doctor picked up his bag and turned to leave, something inside her almost begged him not to go. He was a complete stranger, but at that moment, he seemed like all she had in the world. She'd never felt so alone, and she didn't know if she had the strength she needed to get through this.

"Goodbye, Miss Smith."

"Goodbye, Dr Peters," Florence said, and the moment he closed the door behind him, she sank to her knees and cried.

Queenie had been barely conscious for all of Saturday and most of Sunday. Whenever she came to, she always seemed in pain, and so Florence gave her a little more of the painkilling powders. She realised, of course, that it was the powders to thank for Queenie's unconsciousness, but she knew that it was necessary. She realised that the doctor had left her the medicine as a kindness, to rid Queenie of the pain even if it meant almost sleeping her way through what was left of her life.

Despite it being a cold winter's evening, Florence

had kept the fire so well stacked that the room had begun to feel oppressive. Sooner or later, the wood and coal would run out, and she would have to go and get more. That was if Queenie lasted that long, of course.

Florence sat on the floor in front of the fire, so warm that her face was red, and she stared at the coal bucket. Would that little bucket of fuel really outlive Queenie Smith? The very thought of it was tearing Florence apart. She had to get out of there, just for a few minutes. She had to feel the cold air on her face, she had to escape the awful stuffiness and the heartbreak.

She took down her shawl and crept out through the door, closing it gently behind her. Queenie was in a deep sleep, and Florence was sure she wouldn't wake for the few minutes that she was gone. A few minutes was all she would dare risk, for she couldn't bear the idea of Queenie slipping away while she was gone. She wouldn't let her beloved grandmother die alone, no matter what.

It was past midnight, and the air outside the tenement was cold and still. It wasn't quiet, exactly, for Florence had come to realise that Limehouse was never fully asleep. She could hear the occasional shouts coming from the direction of the Rose and Crown, not to mention running footsteps and an odd whistle in the distance, no doubt a peeler giving chase to some miscreant, alerting his fellow peelers to his position.

For the first time, those curious sounds, always absent in Wimbledon, were something of a comfort. Life was still going on all around her, even if it was going on in a rather grubby, nefarious way. It was still life, and life seemed suddenly so important to her.

Florence wished she hadn't let her mind stray to Wimbledon, for with those thoughts came thoughts of Marcus Daventry. How much she had lost in just six months. Her life in Wimbledon, her security, and her beloved Marcus. And now, to make everything so much worse, she was going to lose Queenie too.

Growing up as she had done, Florence had never imagined a time when she might be entirely alone in the world, fighting for her own survival. How she missed Marcus, their silly games as she'd hung out the washing, their teasing conversations. She missed his beautiful face. His dark hair and those piercing blue eyes.

Of course, life had taught her enough now. Florence knew that she and Marcus could never have been. And now, what would he think of her? The daughter of a prostitute who had been murdered in Whitechapel! What would have been improbable before was impossible now.

Florence sat on the step outside the main door to the tenement building and tipped her head back to look at the stars. It was a cold, clear night, surely one which would produce a little frost, and the stars seemed brighter than they had for a long time. Looking up made the world seem so much bigger than looking around her. The narrow, claustrophobic streets of Limehouse made her feel as if she lived in a tunnel, in a cage even. But something about the sky above and the idea of a larger world made her feel even more alone. Big or small, nobody was coming to help her.

"Florence?" The sudden voice in the darkness made her gasp. A man was standing at the end of the path, a silhouette. "Are you all right?" She realised it was the voice of Jimmy Bates.

"I don't want to argue with you. Please, just leave me alone," Florence said in a defeated tone.

"I don't want to argue either. I want to say I'm sorry." The silhouette spread his arms wide in a placatory manner. "And I *am* sorry, Florence. I was just shocked, and it brought everything back to me. It's not an excuse for all the nasty things I said to you, the nasty things I said to your Grandma, I suppose it's just the reason."

"I'm sorry, I just can't concentrate on this," Florence said, feeling angry with herself for being grateful to see him.

"What's happened?" Jimmy asked gently, taking a few cautious steps towards her. He was staring at her face in the moonlight, and she realised now that he could see just how much crying she'd done.

"Florence?" he went on, closing the gap between them and crouching down on his haunches so that he was at eye level with her.

"It's my Grandma. She's very sick."

"Has she had another turn?"

"It's a bit more than a turn, Jimmy. The doctor says she's dying. She doesn't have very many days left."

"Oh, Florence, I'm so sorry," Jimmy said and moved

to sit next to her on the doorstep, his arm sliding around her shoulders.

Unable to help herself, Florence leaned against him; she needed somebody by her side for a few minutes. She didn't want to be alone anymore. Jimmy was quiet for the longest time, rocking her gently and letting her cry as he kept his protective arm firmly around her shoulders.

"She's done everything in her power to protect me all my life, Jimmy, and now there isn't a single thing I can do to help her."

"You'll be with her, right up until the end. That's the most important thing you can do for another person. Just for them to know that you're there." His words reminded her of the fact that he had attended his own father's hanging as a little boy. Is that what he meant? Had it helped his father in those last moments to know that his son was there for him? It was all so confusing. This was the son of the man who'd murdered Florence's mother, and yet she found herself picturing the little boy standing in the midst of a baying crowd as his father was put to death.

"I really didn't know who you were, Jimmy. And even if I had known, I wouldn't have laughed up my sleeve."

"I know, I shouldn't have said that to you. Your Grandma came at me, you see, wanting me to stay away from you and all. I can't say I blame her, I suppose. But it was a shock, a real shock. Your grandma was angry, but so was I. I was only five when he... Well, you know the rest. I didn't even know he'd done anything wrong when I was a little boy. He was just my father, that's all. I needed him, but he was taken away and killed."

"I *am* sorry for you, Jimmy. Whatever happened between my mother and your father, we didn't really have a say in it, did we?" She was so grateful for his sudden presence that she couldn't find an ounce of dislike or suspicion for him. She could hardly even remember the cruelty of his words on the last day she'd seen him. Florence had never been lower; she had never been more desperate for a friend.

"I suppose we were both victims of it in our own way," he said.

"In the same way. We were just children."

"I really would like to be a friend to you, Florence. I know you don't have any reason to believe it, but I wouldn't dream of hurting you. And you shouldn't be alone, not now, not when you're suffering. If you need me, you know where to find me. And if you need me, I will come. I will come, I promise." She was surprised that he tenderly kissed the top of her head, but she wasn't dismayed by it. It had been a kind and comforting gesture, nothing more.

"Thank you, Jimmy. I'd like to be friends too."

"Then friends we are, Florence."

"I'd better go back in. I only came out for a little air and I don't want to leave Grandma alone for too long."

"All right then," he said and got to his feet, reaching down both hands to take hers and help her up. "As I said, you know where to find me."

"I do, Jimmy. Thank you." She turned to make her way back inside the building. Perhaps it had been fate which had taken her to the doorstep at just the moment Jimmy Bates was passing. Perhaps the sins of the father should not, after all, be visited on the son.

CHAPTER TEN

"I know I said I would work today, Mr Mason, but my grandmother is so terribly ill." Florence was inches away from tears.

"Then you have to get somebody else to look after her, girl. I can't have you trotting away from the mill every time your grandmother takes a turn!" Mr Mason was shouting at her, and Florence felt the purest frustration; why could he not just understand?

"It's not a turn, Mr Mason. Dr Peters came out to her on Saturday after I saw you, and he said that she's dying. She's barely conscious."

"Then she won't realise you're not there, will she?" Mr Mason said heartlessly.

"I don't want her to die alone. Would you let a member of your family die alone for the sake of a day's work?" Florence was furious; how could he have said such an awful thing? Did this man have no heart at all, or had it simply been replaced by a swinging brick?

"One day, girl!" he said, and there was a momentary flash of something in his eyes, perhaps a little remorse. Perhaps a little regret for the poor taste of his words. "If you are not here tomorrow morning, don't come back. Now go!" he said and pointed roughly at the open door of his office.

Florence didn't bother to thank him this time, she just hurried away. How could she possibly be there the following morning? He was expecting Queenie to die on time, on his timetable, for his benefit. But before Florence had time to contemplate the hard-heartedness of the people in Limehouse, she was confronted by yet one more.

Jenny was standing just outside the large wooden doors which lead into the mill room. It was clear that she had been listening at the door, and there was something of a satisfied little smirk on her face.

"Lazing around and leaving me to do everything, that's what you've been doing!" Jenny said harshly.

"Since it's clear you've heard every word of the conversation I just had with Mr Mason, I think you know very well that's not true. My grandmother is dying, but I haven't got time to stand here with you." Florence pushed past so roughly that Jenny, small and skinny, fell against the mill room doors. Florence didn't care, she just kept walking.

"I haven't finished with you yet!" Jenny said, hurrying outside into the cold day after her.

"Well, I'm finished with you." Florence didn't even break her stride.

"I hope your grandmother lives!" Jenny said suddenly, surprising Florence so much that she stopped and turned to look at her. However, she could see instantly that it had been a mistake. Jenny was still not to be trusted, and the broad, unkind smile on her ugly face spoke volumes. "I hope she lives until tomorrow afternoon. That's all, just tomorrow afternoon. Then Mr Mason won't have you back, and I'll never have to see your stupid face or hear your stupid voice again."

Florence stood staring at her for a moment, so utterly flawed by such cruelty. She'd never done anything to Jenny beyond existing, something which the hateful, jealous little girl seemed to object to vehemently. What was it with people of her own class that they liked to see others fall? They liked to see them suffer, to watch them hanging from a rope, all to know that somebody else's life was, at that moment, worse than their own. As far as Florence was concerned, Limehouse was the most hateful place on earth.

"You'd do better to get back in the mill, you little rat before I go in and shout Mr Mason and tell him that you're hanging around outside when you're supposed to be in doing your work!" Once again, Jimmy Bates seemed to appear from nowhere. He advanced upon Jenny and she, obviously seeing something in his expression that Florence missed, looked suddenly afraid and turned on her heel. She ran all the way back to the mill, disappearing through the door before Florence had a chance to draw breath.

"Thank you, Jimmy. *Again*," Florence said and gave

a weak smile. "You always seem to be here when I need you." It was true, although she immediately wished she hadn't said it. It gave too much away, and that was something that Queenie would have urged her to guard against.

"My pleasure, Florence. That's what friends are for," he said and smiled at her, that broad, handsome, cheerful smile that had first made him so appealing. It hardly seemed possible that the cruel and ugly words he had once spoken to her could have come from lips with the ability to smile like that. "Anyway, how is Queenie doing?" he asked, and his smile faded, his face becoming a picture of concern.

"No better. Worse, if I'm honest."

"I suppose that's to be expected. I'm sorry, Florence," he said and reached out to lay a hand on her shoulder. It reminded her, just for a moment, of the way he had seemed to comfort one of the girls he had been speaking to outside the Rose and Crown so many weeks before.

"I'd better get back to her, Jimmy. I hate to leave her alone."

"Of course. Well, like I said, you know where I am."

As Florence hurried back home, she began to wonder if Queenie, ordinarily so good at working out the characters and motives of others, might have been wrong this time. He'd been angry at her, yes. He'd said things she'd never wanted to hear, that was also true. But he'd apologised like a man, and hadn't he suffered just as she had for the want of a parent?

More than anything, Florence wanted to talk to Queenie about it. Queenie had always been the person she turned to for guidance of any kind, but as far as that was concerned, Florence knew that she had lost her already. She couldn't risk worrying her grandmother, not in her final days. No, Florence was just going to have to trust herself from now on. She was going to have to listen to her own instincts and follow her own heart. Queenie couldn't help her anymore.

As Queenie's condition worsened, Florence let go thoughts of everything outside that room of theirs. She forgot about the mill, about Mr Mason, about the rotten Jenny, and even about the kindness of Jimmy Bates.

She forgot her worries, and her fears for the future, because all Florence could see and feel was her own heartbreak as her beloved grandmother slipped away inch by inch.

Queenie hadn't coughed for some days now, and Florence wondered if it was because she was giving up. Although the doctor hadn't spoken of the graveness of her illness within her earshot, Florence thought it likely that Queenie had already known. Feeling her own life starting to slip away, perhaps she had given up trying to cough out the entity which was stuck fast to her lung.

The powders that Dr Peters left with Florence had certainly made Queenie more comfortable, and even though she wished she could have a little more conversation with her in these last days, Florence wouldn't have traded her grandmother's ease for anything. She seemed only to wake now for long enough to look at Florence, her eyes silently begging for more of the medicine. So, when Queenie's voice broke Florence out of her little trance, it was a great surprise.

"Where are you, child?" The voice was tired and weak but clear, and Florence got up from where she had been sitting next to the fire and hurried across the room.

"I'm here, Grandma. I'm right here." Florence sat down on the bed and reached out to take Queenie's hand. However, when she touched her hand, it made Queenie jump a little, and Florence realised that even though her eyes were open, her grandmother could no longer see.

"It's all right, Florence," Queenie said when Florence began to sob. "It's just my time, that's all. I wish I could have looked upon your beautiful face once more though, really, I do. So much like your mother. So many times, these days, I almost call you Gladys. Now you are of an age, you remind me more of her than ever before. To have been able to look at you one last time would have been like looking at you both."

"You'll see her soon, Grandma. You'll be together again. Grandpa will be there too, won't he?" Florence said, as much for her benefit as Queenie's. She knew they didn't have long left together, and the only comfort Florence could draw from it was the idea that Queenie would be reunited with the husband and daughter she had loved so much. She couldn't think about the deeper meaning, about the fact that she would be the one left behind. She could only survive minute by minute.

"I know they'll be there, my sweet. I might not always be at church on a Sunday, but I know they've always told me true. I know where I'm going, and I know who'll be there waiting for me." It was the most Queenie had said for days. "And as much as I will be looking down on you from heaven, Florence, I need to know that you'll keep yourself safe."

"I will, Grandma," Florence said, knowing exactly what her grandmother was referring to; Jimmy Bates. Perhaps not just Jimmy Bates, but any man who might treat her badly.

"Don't you ever go listening to any sweet talk, do you hear me? I know it was never meant to be with you and young Marcus Daventry, and I know you loved him. I know you still do love him, don't you?"

"Yes, I love him. I always will," Florence said, feeling sadder than ever.

"Well, rich or poor, unless a man is as good and as kind as Marcus Daventry, you swear to me you'll turn your back on him." Queenie's voice was suddenly as strong and as fervent as ever it had been. "You swear it to me now, Florence Goodyear." It was the first time that Queenie had called Florence by her real name.

"I swear it, Grandma. I swear it." Florence was sobbing.

"That's all I needed to hear. My girl; my bright girl. Just you remember that. Just remember that you're a clever girl, you can read and write and stand head and shoulders above the crowd. You have it in you to make your own way in this world, never forget it."

"I won't," Florence said, already doubting the veracity of her grandmother's bold statement.

"And always remember you're loved. Death might part us now, but my love for you is eternal."

"And I love you, Grandma. Please don't leave me," Florence said, her voice childlike as she begged. But it was all too late; Queenie had gone.

"I'm sorry, girl, but I have to set an example to the others. If I let you come back now, they'll all be taking days off whenever they feel like it for any old excuse." Mr Mason was clearly not going to bend.

"It wasn't any old excuse, Mr Mason. My grandmother died on Tuesday and I buried her yesterday. I have nobody left in the world now, nobody to look after, nobody to care for. I won't need to take another day off for as long as I work here, Mr Mason, I swear it."

"You won't need to take a day off, girl, because you *do not* work here anymore." Mr Mason had already turned his attention away from her and was studying a pile of papers on his desk. Florence had never felt so diminished, so dismissed and so worthless.

"I worked hard here, Mr Mason. I worked harder than most and I think you know it. Where is your compassion?"

"Compassion doesn't pay the bills."

"But they are not *your* bills, Mr Mason. You manage the mill; you don't own it. The owner doesn't even know who I am, never mind that I had to take some time to spend with my grandmother as she lay dying. The workforce is afraid of you already, you don't need to make an example of me."

"I know you worked hard, but you're not irreplaceable. And I'm getting a little tired of you and your clever ways, thinking you're smarter than I am, even better than I am."

"I don't think anything of the sort."

"Maybe you should go back to Wimbledon. Yes, that's right, I know why you've got such airs about you," he said with an ugly sneer. "You'll certainly fit in better there than you do here. Limehouse isn't the place for you, you'd do better to leave it."

"I can't leave it, not with no job and no money. Mr Mason, I am begging you." Florence felt the tears rolling down her face. "I will have nothing."

"Then you should have thought of that before you decided not to turn up here on Tuesday, shouldn't you?"

"Simple as that, is it?" Florence knew she would get nowhere with him. "Let's hope you can be so practical, that you can draw such fine distinctions when somebody you love is taking their last breaths."

"That's it, get out." Mr Mason got up from behind his desk and began to advance upon her. Florence, somehow resigned to whatever life was going to beat her with next, simply stood there. She didn't even have the energy to be afraid. "Come on, out!"

Mr Mason took her roughly by the arm and began to drag her out of his office. As he pulled her through the corridor, Florence had a fleeting glance at the little window in the great doors to the mill room. The face staring out was unmistakably Jenny's, and the smile was unmistakably cruel and gleeful. A feeling overwhelmed her and she hated Limehouse and every person in it. What foul, ugly creatures they were. How they rolled around and revelled in another's pain, and how much enjoyment they got from such a rotten occupation.

"Oi!" came a shout as Mr Mason dragged her outside. He let go of her suddenly as Jimmy Bates, appearing again just when she needed him. He loomed out of the blue and seized Mr Mason by his lapels. "You get your hands off her, do you hear me?" Jimmy shouted in Mr Mason's face.

Mr Mason, brave when he was handling a young woman so much smaller than him, was less so when he was himself being manhandled by somebody so much larger.

"All right, all right, no need to get your knickers in a twist!" Mr Mason said, aiming for a little cocky bravado, but showing himself up with the look of fear in his eyes. "Jimmy, there's no need for that now, is there?" he went on, something a little pleading in his voice. "There's no need for any unpleasantness, I didn't mean nothing by it."

"I reckon you ought to get yourself back inside the mill before I change my mind and give you the hiding you deserve." There was something menacing in Jimmy's tone, but Florence was just too exhausted and devastated to dwell on it.

"You didn't come to find me, Florence," Jimmy said, once Mason had taken himself back to the relative safety of the textile mill. "She's gone, isn't she?" He stood in front of her, those pale blue eyes staring right into hers.

"I just didn't want to leave her, Jimmy. I didn't want to leave her for a single minute, not even after she'd gone. It was hard enough to run down for the undertaker, and I ran all the way back. She was dead, but still, I didn't want to leave her there on her own."

"And the funeral?"

"It was yesterday. I was the only one there, save for the vicar, but I just couldn't think straight."

"You've got nothing to be sorry about, Florence. I understand, I really do." Suddenly he put his arms around her and pulled her in close. "Did you manage to give her a good send-off?"

"As best I could with what I had. Grandma was too proud to have been dumped in a pauper's grave, so I use the last of her gin money to bury her."

"Something tells me old Queenie would have preferred you kept that gin money for yourself, I think you're going to need it," he said and cast his eyes back in the direction of the textile mill. "I take it they finished you there?"

"For the crime of taking time away from the mill to spend with my dying grandmother, yes." She shook her head sadly. "But that's Limehouse for you."

"That's London for you. More of London is like this

than not, Florence. More folk are hard and cruel than not. I wish you weren't just finding that out now. I'm glad for you that you had a nice place to grow up in. You're clever and gentle, but that only makes me worry about you more. Limehouse is no place for someone as good as you."

"Funny, Mr Mason just said the same thing, although he didn't put it so kindly."

"I didn't mean that you're not welcome here," he said and held her tighter still as he gave a little laugh. "I just mean that it's no place for a girl like you to be alone in, that's all. But you're not alone, Florence. I promise you, you're not alone."

"Thank you, Jimmy." She closed her eyes and felt relieved and dismayed at the same time.

Jimmy's kindness was much needed, his arms around her most welcome, but he wasn't Marcus Daventry and he never would be. And so, as she stood there in his arms, Florence found herself imagining that she was back in Wimbledon, standing in the yard, a linen basket by her feet. She imagined the arms around her now were those of Marcus, and it was the greatest comfort she could ever have known.

CHAPTER ELEVEN

*F*lorence sat on the floor in front of the empty fire grate. She'd cleaned it out earlier and scrubbed it, needing the distraction. There was no sense in leaving it, she didn't have a stitch of wood to put on it now. She'd used every last piece in keeping Queenie warm, and the fact that she was frozen to the bone now could not have made her regret it for a second.

Florence had spent the rest of the day there in that room, not moving from it once. The fact that she lost her job at the mill hadn't come as a surprise, not really, but it had made her feel more hopeless and alone, and she wanted to be in the last place she'd felt her grandmother's embrace.

The gentle tap at the door startled her so badly that she cried out. It was late, surely past midnight, who on earth would be calling on her now? It couldn't be the landlord; his money wasn't due for some days yet. Florence sat frozen, afraid, alone. Queenie would have marched right up to the door and bellowed through it, demanding to know who on earth thought it was a good idea to knock so late at night. But Florence wasn't Queenie, and Queenie wasn't here anymore.

"Florence? It's me. It's Jimmy," he whispered through the door, tapping lightly on it again.

Florence got up and crossed the room, opening the door to him, her hand spread flat on her chest as if to hold in her pounding heart.

"Sorry, you startled me. I couldn't imagine who it would be."

"I know it's late, but I couldn't stop thinking about you. I don't know, I suppose I knew in here that you'd still be wide-awake," he said, and tapped his own chest. "I've brought you a few bits. It looked to me like you hadn't eaten for days when I saw you earlier. You've got to keep your strength up now, Queenie would want that." He held out a heavy-looking loaf of bread, and a large cube wrapped in paper which could only be cheese. "Nothing fancy, but it will keep you going." He smiled, and Florence stood back to let him in.

He walked into the room, his head turning this way and that as he took in the place which had housed Florence and Queenie for more than six months. Florence was glad that she had everything tidy, that she had gone down to the little room with the sink and the water pump in the basement and pounded the bedsheets against a washboard until her fingers were raw. Queenie wouldn't have liked anybody to see the blood she had coughed up, even if she wasn't there to feel the embarrassment herself. In death, Florence had done her grandmother proud.

"It's not much, but it's already more than I can afford," Florence said and gave a mirthless laugh. "Thank you for coming, Jimmy. Thank you for the bread and cheese."

"It's the very least I can do," he said and set the items down on the table. "Although I should have brought you some firewood, it's colder in here than it is outside."

"I used the last of the wood keeping Gran warm."

"Then I should be warm enough in the same room as your heart, Florence," he said, and took down her grandmother's shawl from a hook by the door and wrapped it around her. "Here, sit down for a minute."

The two of them sat down at the wooden table, and Florence suddenly felt exhausted. Just having Jimmy there relaxed her enough that she finally felt tired, but she knew that she couldn't just climb into bed and go to sleep now, not when he'd made such an effort, not when he'd brought her bread and cheese.

"I just don't know what to do next. A part of me wants to run all the way back to Wimbledon, but there's nothing for me there anymore. The family that Gran and I worked for are long gone, and who would take me on? It would be too much of a risk. But then staying here is a risk."

"How is it?" Jimmy asked and lightly patted her hand.

"Because I don't have a job here either. The mill was my best hope, but that's all gone now. There are no houses here good enough to have servants inside, even rough, low paid servants."

"What are you going to do?"

"I'll try the shops. There are a few shops here in Limehouse, perhaps one of them needs somebody. Perhaps one of them will have a place for me."

"I wouldn't get your hopes up," Jimmy said prophetically. "Sorry, I don't want to make you feel worse, really I don't, but I don't want you having false hope either. Even the folks with businesses in Limehouse, save for the mill, are down on their uppers. There isn't any money here."

"You work, Jimmy. What is it you told me? You do any job that comes along. A little bit of this and a little bit of that," Florence said, and suddenly felt a little of her determination returning. "Well, I could do that. I could do what you do."

"You would?" Jimmy said, seeming curiously pleased. "I didn't think so, I must be honest."

"I would. Just tell me what it is you do, Jimmy."

"Ah," he said and pursed his lips for a moment before continuing. "I suppose I thought you knew. I suppose I thought Queenie might have told you."

"How would Queenie have known?" Florence wasn't just tired; she was mentally exhausted. She couldn't put two and two together.

"Well, she made it her business to find out all about me, I suppose."

"What sort of work is it? Can I not do it?"

"Not only could you do it, but you'd make good money at it."

"At what?"

"I think you know what, Florence," he said, and he narrowed his eyes in a way which made her feel suddenly uncomfortable.

"What?"

"Well, the same kind of thing that your mother did. And don't look like that, she got by, didn't she?" he said, suddenly defensive.

"And that's what you do? You send women and girls out to...?" Florence felt sick. She closed her eyes and dropped her head into her hands. "No."

"No?" Jimmy said, and there was suddenly an edge to his voice. "Look, I've come here to do you a good turn, it won't do you any favours to be all hoity-toity about it."

"Hoity-toity? You think not wanting to be used by men for money is hoity-toity, do you?"

"So, here we go again." Jimmy tutted loudly and shook his head. "It's been clear to me for some time that you were going to need my help sooner or later."

"Your help? You mean *this* is why you've been so nice to me? You wanted me to work for you?" Florence looked up, her face full of scorn and disapproval. Her expression made him angry, and she remembered the day that Queenie had leaned over and clicked her fingers loudly in her ear, telling her that Warren Bates, Jimmy's father, could be nice one moment and murderous the next. It could all happen in the click of her fingers.

"Not just for my own sake, but yours too. It's not like

you won't be earning out of it, Florence. In fact, I'll see to it that you get more than you used to get at the mill, and you won't have to work such long hours either."

"I can't believe you're talking about this as if it's an actual possibility," Florence said sternly.

"Just who the hell do you think you're talking to? I came here to help you, just you watch your tone of voice, Florence Goodyear."

"How can you be like that? How can you be so kind, so believably caring, and then so cruel? My grandmother was right about you. You really are a chip off the old block, aren't you?"

"Well, if I am, maybe you ought to be a little less lippy and a little bit more afraid, hadn't you?" he said, leaning across the table at her, those pale blue eyes no longer attractive but frightening and cold. Was he really threatening to murder her the way his father had murdered her mother?

"I should have listened to her," Florence said, getting to her feet and picking up the loaf of bread and the cheese. "Thank you for bringing these to me, Jimmy, but I have no need for them. I'd like you to leave now." He remained seated for almost a minute, and Florence had the awful feeling that his anger was about to boil over.

When he finally stood, he stood so abruptly that Florence leapt back. He sneered at her, snatching the bread and cheese from her hands and turning to walk away.

"I'm going to let this go, for now, Florence, but only because I know that you will come back to me. You might be nursing your finer feelings at the moment, and I suppose I ought to give you the chance at least to get over Queenie's passing, but once you're thinking straight again, you'll be back."

"I won't. I can promise you, Jimmy Bates, that I won't make the same mistakes that my mother made. Sorry, but we can't be friends anymore."

"You will be back," Jimmy said, and the sneer disappeared to be replaced by a cocky, confident smile. However, he could smile all he liked, he would never be that bright and handsome young man again. He'd never been that bright and handsome young man in the first place. "When you're hungry enough, you'll come crawling."

"I'll never crawl to you, Jimmy. I'll never crawl to anybody."

"We'll see," Jimmy said and opened the door. He strode out through it, arrogantly not bothering to even close it behind him.

The moment he was gone, Florence ran to the door and shut it, throwing the bolts across. She leaned against it breathing heavily, tears streaming down her face. How could she have been such a fool? Of course, her Grandma knew what he was, of course, she did! Queenie had seen it all before, and she had lost so much to a man just like Jimmy Bates.

Florence slid down the door, drawing her knees up to her chest and wrapping her arms around them, crying like a child. She was truly alone now, her heart both hating Jimmy Bates and missing that friendship he had given her, even if that friendship had been built on a lie. Lie or not, it had made her feel less alone. But now she was truly alone, completely alone, with no one in the world and nowhere to go.

"Marcus, why did everything have to change? Why did Everything have to fall apart? I miss you so much. I would give anything, anything to have my world back again. To have you, to have Grandma, to have Wimbledon." But even as she spoke the words, Florence knew that it was useless. She could never go back, and nothing would ever be right again.

CHAPTER TWELVE

*N*obody was hiring. Florence had trudged the streets of Limehouse asking for work to no avail. After being awake all night, grieving for her grandmother and shocked, once again, by the appalling behaviour of Jimmy Bates, Florence was certain she didn't look her best. The skin around her eyes was red and raw from crying, her cheeks hollowed out from days and days of not eating properly.

The problem was, she knew that she didn't have time to waste, and when the sun had risen that morning, it seemed to have awakened her sense of purpose. She needed to find work and fast, or the landlord would throw her out on the streets. She knew this to be true; she'd seen other tenants suffer that very fate.

As it was, she probably wouldn't be able to find a job that would pay the entire rent. Even if they accepted her back at the mill, it didn't quite cover it. As much as Queenie's little gin-making industry had worried Florence, it had been absolutely crucial to their survival. Florence wished now that she'd paid attention, that she'd learned how to make gin for herself. She'd risk anything now just to keep going. Well, almost anything.

She was beginning to understand more and more what had led her mother down the path which took her straight to Warren Bates. This was the first time in her life she'd experienced true poverty, and if she had been raised in it, as her mother was, she might have considered Jimmy Bates' offer something of a lifeline.

Hours later, standing in one of the wider streets in Limehouse, Florence realised that she just didn't know what to do next. She'd tried every shop, she was sure of it, and she could feel all hope slipping away. Turning to make her way back home again, deciding to rest her head in the safety of her room whilst she still had it, Florence saw one tiny shop on a corner that she realised she hadn't tried.

Hurrying over, she saw that it was in something of a poor state of repair. There were large windows on the two sides of the corner, and peering in, Florence could see an elderly lady sitting at a table at the back of the shop, some spectacles perched on the end of her nose as she squinted at her sewing.

There wasn't much else to be seen but that, and Florence quickly realised that it was a repair shop of sorts. The old lady was making repairs to somebody's old clothes. Whilst she was excellent with needle and thread, having been taught well by Mrs Daventry, Florence didn't hold out much hope of the old lady having something for her. Nonetheless, she had to try, and so she pushed open the door and made her way inside.

"Good morning," Florence said brightly. "Good morning," she said a little more loudly when it seemed the old dear hadn't heard her.

"Oh, hello my dear," the lady said in a voice made tremulous with age. "What can I do for you?"

"I was wondering if you might have any work, I really am very good at sewing and making repairs."

"Oh, I do wish I had something for you, really. It would be nice to have the company if I'm honest. But I'm afraid I barely manage myself," the lady said, her face lined and her eyes sweet and apologetic.

Looking around, Florence could see that it was true. There were a few bits and pieces of clothes on the table for the woman to attend to, but very little else in the shop. Wooden shelves lined the walls, but there was nothing on them save for a thick layer of dust that the ageing lady likely couldn't see or if she could, was too frail to do anything about. For a moment, Florence felt sorrier for the old lady than she did for herself.

"Thank you anyway, I appreciate your kindness," Florence said truthfully. Every other person she had spoken to that day had been gruff and abrupt, almost no humanity about them at all. This lady was different, and at least if her day had been unsuccessful, it had ended on a kindly note.

"I do wish you well, my dear. This is a very tough place and you seem to have been nicely raised."

"Thank you, and you're right, this is a very tough place." Florence nodded, thinking that the lady, although clearly born and raised in Limehouse if her accent was anything to go by, had a certain gentleness about her too.

She was old, even older than Queenie had been, and her character was a thousand miles away. She didn't have Queenie's wonderful brashness, that bustling determination. She had a gentle expression and a sort of calmness. If only Florence could have found some work with this nice lady. How wonderful that would have been.

"If you get stuck, perhaps you could try the mill. They always seem to be hiring."

"I'm afraid they already turned me out of there."

"I've heard they're not very pleasant."

"No, not pleasant at all. Well, thank you for hearing me out." Florence was already turning to leave.

"I wish you the best of luck. You'll find something soon, I'm sure of it."

As Florence walked away from the little sewing shop, she was equally sure that she would never find anything. Perhaps she should leave Limehouse after all. But where would she go? And who would take her on once she had become homeless?

As she walked the dark depressing streets, Florence had the awful sensation of time running out.

Florence had managed to successfully evade the landlord for the better part of the month, but finally, he caught up with her. She'd sold most of her grandmother's things, her good dresses, and the fine wooden trunks that they had moved their belongings from Wimbledon in. She hadn't got much for them, but at least she'd been able to eat. However, there wasn't enough to pay the rent, something which she finally had to admit to the landlord when he caught up with her at last.

Florence had packed her own things into a large bag, and still having three good dresses and a nice apron, not to mention two good nightgowns, it was rather cumbersome. Still, she realised that these clothes would have to last her for years, now, so she couldn't afford to let anything go. She had nothing of her grandma now, not even a keepsake, and as the landlord walked her from the room, Florence realised that she didn't even have that now. Her memories of her grandmother in that room laughing and chattering as she made her gin were all she had left. How long would it be before those memories faded when she was no longer in that room but living on the streets?

"Out you go, onto the streets, like you deserve," the landlord said, giving her an unnecessary shove from the boundary of his property and onto the pavement.

Florence was too tired and too downhearted to even argue with him. What sort of man thought anybody deserved to be on the streets? A Limehouse man, that was who! Apart from Dr Peters who had been so kind to Queenie, and the old lady in the sewing shop who had at least treated her with respect, there wasn't another decent soul in that godforsaken place.

Florence stood for a moment looking all around her, realising that there wasn't a single thing for her in Limehouse, and now that she had no home, what reason was there for her to stay? It was late afternoon, far too late to start walking to another place. And she knew she would be walking a long way because she wanted to leave the grime and ugliness of places like Limehouse and Whitechapel far behind her.

So, in the end, she realised that she would have to find somewhere safe to sleep that night until it was time for her to leave when the sun came up the next morning.

It was dusk now, rather than dark, and she wanted to find a quiet alleyway somewhere to hide out of the way before the people who roamed the streets of Limehouse by night came out. She idly wondered if she would survive until morning, for it was December now and bitingly cold.

A few streets from the Rose and Crown, Florence found a narrow gap between two shops. It wasn't a through alleyway, for it ended in a wall, a dead end. It was very narrow, and she couldn't see any signs that others had slept there. Perhaps this would be the very place for her. She picked her way through the falling darkness, deciding that she would be better all the way up the far end out of sight.

However, upon reaching it, she had an awful feeling of being trapped, being vulnerable, and she turned around deciding to find somewhere else. When she walked directly into a man who had crept up behind her, Florence cried out. The man immediately hit her hard across the face, something between a slap and a punch. It knocked her against the dead end, and she bumped her head on the wall, although not so hard as to do her any damage. She opened her mouth to cry out again, but the man balled his fist this time and raised it high, threatening to strike. Florence remained silent, holding a hand out in front of her, pleading with her eyes for the man to leave her alone.

"I don't want anything from you but the bag," the man said as if to spare her the indignity of a sexual assault was somehow a favour when he had clearly chosen to relieve her of her last few belongings. *What a gentleman!*

"It's all I have in the world."

"And in a moment, it will be all I have in the world. Hand it over, or you'll be sorry." The man was gruff, thickset, and he wreaked of strong liquor.

Florence suddenly became belligerent; why should she let go of all she had just so that this man could spend the night in the Rose and Crown drinking it all away?

"But it is just clothes, that's all. What on earth would you want with my dresses?" Florence said, but she knew exactly what he wanted with them; he didn't care what was in the bag, as long as it was something that could be sold for a few coins and feed his addiction.

The man had clearly chosen not to listen to another word, and he reached out and roughly took the bag from her. Florence had tried to hold on, but he'd easily pushed her away and she had crashed against the wall once again.

The man turned to leave, and Florence cried out again, this time in surprise when he dropped to the floor. Somebody in the alleyway had hit him and hit him hard enough to knock him out. In the darkness of the alleyway, she could just make out a man who was picking up her bag from the floor and closing the gap between them.

"Here," the man said, and she recognised his voice immediately.

"Jimmy?" she said and was both relieved and dismayed all at once.

He was always there when she needed him, but Florence had worked it out now. It was by design. Jimmy Bates, despite the veneer of affability, was a sharp and shrewd operator. He was a man who easily spotted people's vulnerability, and he played on them. He made sure he was always the man to rescue her from trouble, thereby making himself a figure of stability in her world. Was that how he got other girls to work for him? She was reminded of the days she had seen him comforting the girl outside the Rose and Crown. He had his hands on her shoulders and was looking into her face. He was making her feel cared for when the truth was that she was anything but cared for. That poor girl was just Jimmy Bates' meal ticket, and his pretence at goodness and caring was just a mockery.

"So, this is where you live now, is it?" he said, and she said could see him more clearly now that her eyes had begun to adjust to the gloom. "It's not safe for you here, Florence."

"I realise that now," Florence said, wanting to avoid an argument with him before she was clear of that alleyway. She didn't want to jump out of the frying pan and straight into the fire, after all.

She reached out and took the bag, smiling at him gently and nodding her thanks. She was relieved when he turned to walk out of the alleyway, and she could do no other than follow him. She just needed to be clear of it, that was all.

"When did your landlord kick you out, then?" he asked when the two of them had made their way out onto the main street.

"Just an hour ago."

"He couldn't wait until daylight?" Jimmy said and seemed truly scandalised by that. It was easy now to see why she had been so taken in by him. There were moments in which she was certain he was genuine. He had his own set of standards and turning somebody out in the darkness instead of the light was just beyond the pale for him. And yet convincing girls to lay down with strange men and let them have their way apparently was not. What a curious jumble of a man he was. Perhaps it was this very nature which made him truly dangerous.

"It's not safe out here for a girl like you, Florence."

He held his hands up as if in some sort of surrender. "I'm not going to start with the miss snooty business again, I promise. You do stand out, I told you that before. You're just gentler, more decent, and it's a good thing, really it is. But out here, on the streets at night, it just makes you prey."

Prey to whom if not Jimmy Bates?

"I'm going to leave Limehouse for good." Florence wanted him to know, in the gentlest way possible, that she would never, ever work for him. "As soon as it's light, I'm going."

"Where?"

"I don't know. Just somewhere that isn't so miserable, dirty and without an ounce of humanity."

"I don't blame you. But let's get you off the street for tonight at least, shall we?" he said, and there it was again that genuine concern. But it wasn't, was it? This was Jimmy Bates not yet ready to give up, she was sure of it.

"Where?" Florence said, wondering if she could manage for one night. If she could keep Jimmy in a good temper until morning, might it not be worth it for somewhere to rest that night that wasn't a Limehouse alley?

"I've got a place you can stay. I have a couple of rooms over the Rose and Crown now." He smiled and shrugged amiably.

A couple of rooms above the Rose and Crown. It chilled Florence to the bone as she remembered how Queenie had told her that Warren Bates had rooms over the Dog and Duck in Whitechapel. Rooms in which Gladys Goodyear had the life choked out of her. She had an awful sense that if she went with him now, she would be allowing history to repeat itself.

"That's kind, but no thank you," she said but she could hear the panic in her voice.

"Here we go again!" Jimmy said, and once again she heard Queenie's fingers snap by her ear. His mood has changed in a heartbeat. "Just do as you're told for once," he went on and roughly snatched her arm.

Florence tried to pull away from him, but Jimmy held her fast.

"I'm not going to be what you want me to be, Jimmy. Just let me go, just leave me alone," she shouted.

"No, I've had enough of your nonsense. I've had enough of you thinking you're better than everybody else, the daughter of a prostitute, no less! Well, I'll make one of you before this night is over!"

Her terror was almost enough to render her unconscious as she felt her feet slipping and sliding, unable to resist that terrible strength of his. Knowing that she would have to do something, Florence kicked him as hard in the knee as she possibly could.

She'd hit him in just the right place, for he dropped like a stone in a pond, clutching his knee and swearing and cursing inventively. Knowing that she didn't have a moment to lose, she held her bag tightly to her chest and ran as if the devil himself were chasing her. She ran and ran until she heard his shouts behind her, his heavy footfalls. He had recovered himself enough to give chase, and Florence had never been more frightened in her entire life.

Seeing a pale light in the distance, Florence headed for it. It was a shop, and it was still open. If she ran in there, surely, he wouldn't dare to follow?

No sooner had she burst in through the door than she realised she was standing in the same little sewing repair shop where she had tried to find work just weeks before. The old lady was sitting at her table, trying to make her repairs by the light of a single oil lamp. She looked up at Florence, startled, and then pushed her spectacles up her nose and peered out into the street beyond.

Seeing Jimmy Bates giving chase, the old lady was on her feet in an instant, and she made her way to the front door of her shop with surprising speed. It took a moment for Florence to realise that the woman had picked up a wooden broom en route, and was now brandishing it fearlessly as Jimmy approached, breathless and furious.

"You won't take a step over this threshold, Jimmy Bates, or you'll feel the sharp end of this broom, and I'll have the peelers on you without a second thought!" The voice was still thin and reedy, but there was a determination in it which not only surprised Florence but seemed to bring Jimmy up short. "That's right, you know I'll do it. I'm not afraid of you, Jimmy, you're no better than that father of yours. Sooner they catch up with you the way they caught up with him, the better. I know what you are.

Everybody knows what you are. Get out of here, or I'll shout loud enough to bring out the whole street. Folk aren't as charmed by you as you seem to think they are. They're already getting tired of you and your big-wig ways. Now get!" The old woman thrust the broom out so sharply that Jimmy was forced to jump backwards.

Florence could do no more than look on in sheer surprise as Jimmy, after a final glare in her direction, turned and walked away. Perhaps this delicate old woman was much more like Queenie than Florence had given her credit for.

As Jimmy walked away into the darkness, the old lady closed and bolted the door behind him.

"Now, let's see if I have a little something to drink. Something that will steady your nerves, my dear," she said, putting the broom down and smiling at Florence.

CHAPTER THIRTEEN

Florence winced as the brandy slid down her throat, warming her insides. At least it wasn't gin. She knew by instinct that she couldn't abide the stuff.

"It can be a little warming, my dear. It's an old bottle, too, I can hardly remember the last time I needed a drop to steady my nerves," the old lady said and smiled. At least she wasn't a gin-soaked disaster like so many others in Limehouse were. "My name is Winnie, by the way. Winnie Gibbons."

"It's nice to meet you, Mrs Gibbons."

"Oh please, call me Winnie. And what's your name, young lady?"

"Florence. Florence Smith," Florence said and hesitated. "At least I thought it was Florence Smith for a long time. My name is actually Florence Goodyear."

"That's intriguing," Winnie said and laughed. "I thought you were likely an interesting young person when you first came into my shop. Mind you, I hadn't expected you to come tearing in with Jimmy Bates hot on your heels, I must admit."

"I don't work for him; I wouldn't want you to think that. You obviously know what he is, although I must admit I was surprised to find it out myself."

"Yes, he's charming, isn't he? His father was the same way."

"You knew Warren Bates?" Florence asked, and took another sip of the brandy.

"I knew *of* him. Limehouse, Whitechapel, everybody crosses paths with everybody else in the end. I wasn't at all surprised to find out his son had turned out to be exactly the same."

"One moment he's pleasant, the next he's murderous."

"And that would make him even more like his father," Winnie said and sat down at her table again. "Sit yourself down, my dear."

"My mother was the woman Warren Bates murdered. The woman he hanged for," Florence said, the truth pouring out of her before she had even decided to say a word.

"Oh, I am sorry. Although I thought I recognised the name. Goodyear. Gladys Goodyear, wasn't it?"

"Yes, my mother was Gladys Goodyear."

"I didn't know her, I'm afraid, but being as old as I am, I remember all the stories of these places. It was in the papers, you know. It was a big case, and there were plenty at his hanging, so I understand. I didn't go myself, I don't like that sort of thing," Winnie said and shuddered, making Florence like her all the more.

"Me either," Florence said and smiled.

"So, you're the little child that was left behind. I'd followed it all in the newspapers back then, and I must admit that I had often wondered what had become of you. Well, whatever did happen, you have been raised nicely."

"I lived with my grandmother in Wimbledon," Florence began and decided to tell this kindly and brave woman everything. It was the least she could do after Winnie had saved her from Jimmy Bates.

Winnie sat enthralled through the whole thing, smiling romantically every time Florence spoke of Marcus Daventry, smiling sadly when she spoke of the life she and Queenie had been forced to live in Limehouse.

"So, what are you going to do now?" Winnie asked when Florence had come to the end of her tale.

"I suppose I'll try to find another place. I've searched for work all over Limehouse, but there's nothing for me here."

"It worries me that a nice girl like you will be wandering the streets alone. Now I know I said that I didn't have any work for you, and that remains true, but there is a little room at the back of the shop and you may stay there for as long as you like. I can't give you any money, or even any food, I hardly have any to spare. Perhaps a little bread, but nothing more."

"Oh, Mrs Gibbons, that's really so kind of you. I would be so grateful for somewhere to sleep. It would give me time to work out what I ought to do next."

"You're a sensible young woman. I reckon your grandmother raised you well."

"She did, Mrs Gibbons."

"Please, we're friends now, aren't we? You must call me Winnie," Winnie said and picked up her sewing again. "I must admit, I shall be glad of the company. It's something of a lonely life here."

"Here, let me help," Florence said, putting down the empty brandy glass and picking up one of the shirts on the table for mending.

Within a few short weeks, Florence was beginning to feel optimistic again. Determined to repay Winnie's kindness, she had gone out of her way to make herself useful. While she went out most days for an hour or two looking for work, she made sure to spend the rest of her day doing things for Winnie. She tidied up the shop, dusting down the shelves and giving the floor a good sweep and clean. She cleaned the windows, and washed down the blackened woodwork on the outside, revealing a nicely painted old sign which read *Gibbons Sewing Repairs*.

Still having a few coins left from the sale of Queenie's possessions, Florence was able to buy some bread and a few vegetables every day. Winnie had allowed her upstairs, and Florence had been saddened by the impoverished little room that had apparently been Winnie's home ever since her husband had died almost forty years earlier.

There was a stove, however, and Florence made good use of it every day. She prepared hearty stews with the vegetable she brought at the market, and Winnie, who enjoyed the stews greatly, began to seem a little less frail on account of them.

Florence helped in the shop, even though she insisted that Winnie need not pay her. She helped with the sewing, and Winnie was able to take in twice or even three times as much work as she used to.

"I'll have to pay you, Florence. I really cannot live with myself making all this extra money on account of your hard work and not giving you a thing," Winnie said to her one day as the two of them sat side-by-side at the table, companionably sewing.

"It's the least I can do, Winnie. You've put a roof over my head, I can't ask for more than that."

"But you can't have much money left now to keep going out and buying vegetables and bread. From now on, I will pay for the food. And don't argue young lady, I'm in a much better position now with you here than I have been in a very long time. And I'm not so batty that I don't realise you're doing twice as much sewing as me, if not more."

"I like to sew, Winnie. Mrs Daventry taught me when I was a little girl."

"This Mrs Daventry of yours sounds like a nice lady. I reckon your grandmother was right; you really did fall on your feet there."

"And I feel as if I've fallen on my feet again, Winnie."

"This is hardly a fine house in Wimbledon," Winnie

said and laughed, pushing her spectacles up her nose as was her habit.

"It doesn't matter, it feels like home, and that's what makes it exactly the same."

"Even staying in that awful little room at the back of the shop?" Winnie looked over her shoulder.

"There's nothing awful about it," Florence said firmly and thought about all the little changes she had made.

She'd cleaned the place up and tidied it, making herself a comfortable little bed from the blankets and pillows that Winnie had brought down from upstairs. It was more of a nest than a bed, and Florence felt safe there.

"I must admit, even my little room upstairs feels like home again. Thank you for tidying it up and cleaning the floor. I'm not as sprightly as I used to be, and I'm always careful to save my strength for fending off dubious young men at the door with a broom." Winnie laughed, and Florence laughed too. It was the first time she'd laughed genuinely since Queenie had died, and her newfound friendship felt safe and wonderful.

Winnie would have been a fine replacement for Queenie, only she was very different. She was gentler and sweeter, more tolerant of tales of the heart, of talk of feelings and fears. She was becoming important to Florence in her own right, not as a replacement for her beloved grandmother.

"Do you never think of trying to find that young Marcus? Where did he move to in Bedfordshire?"

"Someplace called Ampthill. At least I think that's what it was called. I'd never heard of it."

"Oh yes, I've never been, but it's a nice place out in the country, I believe. There's some tale of a golden hare being hidden out somewhere in a fine park. I can't remember the story really... if I ever truly knew it in the first place. But anyway, you can be pleased that your young man lives in a nice place."

"I don't think I would dare to try to contact him now. So much has happened, and I've found out so much about myself, about my origins, that I can't imagine he would want to know me now."

"People can be very surprising, Florence. I wouldn't give up on him so easily if I were you. After all, you were friends for a reason in the first place, weren't you? Real friends don't turn their backs so easily."

"It would be nice to think so," Florence said and wished rather than hoped that that was true. Marcus was a wonderful young man, but he would have to be truly exceptional to be able to accept the story of her past.

"Now what's that you're working on?" Winnie said, peering at the sewing that Florence had laid on the table. "That's not a repair, is it?"

"No, it's not a repair," Florence said cautiously. "I hope you don't mind, but I found a bolt of fabric in the backroom when I was moving things around, and I thought I would try to make a dress out of it."

"Well goodness me!" Winnie said, clearly impressed. "And of course, I don't mind. There's more fabric up in the attic, stuff I haven't set eyes on for years. I was always better at repairs than making things from scratch, so I abandoned that idea long since."

"I like to make things from scratch."

"You deserve a pretty little dress," Winnie said and smiled warmly.

"Oh no, it isn't for me," Florence said, suddenly more confident and excited about the little ideas she'd had. "It's to sell in the shop."

"A brand-new dress to sell in the shop?" Winnie said as if the idea was somehow earthshattering.

"It's worth a try, isn't it?" Florence was feeling more and more excited. "And I've seen an old tailor's dummy in a thrift shop. I have enough money left to buy it. I thought I could put the dress on the dummy once it's finished and display it in the window."

"My word, you are a revelation, Florence Goodyear!" Winnie said and beamed with pride. "But I insist that you buy that tailor's dummy out of the money made here in the shop. You're not to use your last few coins, do you hear me?"

"I hear you," Florence said, and smiled, a feeling of wonderful contentment washing over her.

CHAPTER FOURTEEN

2 years later.

"I've heard that you can get good dresses in here for cheap!" The young woman marched into the shop, hardly looking at Florence as she began to study the rail of dresses that hung just behind the display in the window.

She had a real Limehouse manner; brash, to the point, and without a single pleasantry.

"Yes, you've heard right," Florence said, and then studied the woman a little more closely. Her mouth fell open when she realised that it was Jenny, the horrid little girl she'd worked with at the textile mill.

She was two years older, just a little taller than she had been, but it was unmistakably her. Her pale skin told Florence most exactly that she still worked at the mill, hidden away from the sunlight day in day out for the better part of the week.

Jenny must be sixteen now, the same as Florence, and yet somehow, she looked older, worn out. Her life was taking a toll on her, and Florence realised that it didn't give her a moment's pleasure to see it. Jenny was unpleasant, she probably always would be, and yet still Florence found room in her heart for a little pity. That could have been her; every day spent in that awful place, making barely enough to survive, being so tired at the end of it that life seemed a pointless exercise.

"You're more than welcome to try something on, and I can adjust it to fit you at no extra charge. The price you see is the price you pay. There's nothing hidden," Florence said, trying to be helpful. Jenny spun around and stared at her.

"Well, I never!" Jenny said, her eyes wide. "I thought I recognised that posh little voice!"

"How are you, Jenny?" Florence asked and smiled, determined to rise above any attempt at antagonism.

"Same as ever, what do you think?" Jenny said, scowling before turning back to the dresses. Well, at least she wasn't going to turn on her heel and march out. Florence might not be keen on Jenny, but she wasn't about to turn away business if she could possibly help it.

In the two years that she had been with Winnie, the shop had come on in leaps and bounds. Her simple but well-made dresses, suitable for work or church, had become something of a hit in the area. Women came not only from Limehouse but Whitechapel too. It was an affordable place for a woman who worked, or a woman with a husband, to be able to buy something new, something which had never been worn by anybody else. Florence knew that that, above anything else, had been part of the draw for many. The women who came into the shop to look at the dresses were women who had never worn something that hadn't been worn by somebody else for several years first.

The shop itself had been transformed; Florence had

used a little of the money they made in the last two years to have a man clean up the outside of the building. He'd washed down the blackened brickwork until it was red again, and he had repaired and painted the window frames and even made a brand-new and very smart wooden sign. It was now called *Gibbons Clothing and Repairs*, a nod to the fact that the larger part of their business now came from the sale of new clothing.

Winnie had given Florence free rein, quickly realising that the young woman was educated enough to make a success of things. Florence went to Finchley regularly to find good, affordable fabric. She worked from morning till night creating dresses of all sizes, simply cut things that could be easily altered to fit the wearer perfectly.

She even took a wage now, given that the shop was making more money than it had ever done. And Winnie, that adorable old woman, worked only a couple of days a week now. She continued to do a little sewing repair sitting at her table, but Florence knew that it was for the pure enjoyment of sitting with her young companion and passing the time.

"I like this one," Jenny said, instantly forgetting her aggression for a moment, as was part of that complicated personality Florence remembered of old.

"Yes, I like that fabric too. The flowers are nice, but it's not so light that it'll show every mark," Florence said conversationally, being practical and pleasant, every bit the shopkeeper.

"I want to try it on," Jenny said roughly.

"Yes, of course," Florence said, maintaining her bright smile. "There's a curtain here, just pop the dress on and let me know when you're in it. I'll come and see what needs to be adjusted if you find you like it."

"Thank you," Jenny said, and attempted a smile as Florence showed her into the curtained off area.

In no time at all, Jenny had the dress on, sweeping the curtain back herself and standing there with her arms spread wide.

"Well, what you think?" Jenny asked, surprising Florence by asking for her opinion.

"The fabric certainly suits you, as does the cut," Florence said truthfully. "I'd need to take it in a little at the waist to make it fit right. Not so much as to make it uncomfortable, but just enough," she went on.

"Then I'll have it," Jenny said and nodded. "When will it be ready?"

"I can have it ready for you tomorrow," Florence said, taking her tape measure from around her neck and picking up a little pottery dish of pins.

"As quick as that?" Jenny said and seemed impressed.

"As quick as that," Florence said and smiled before setting to work with her tape measure and pins.

Florence quickly pinned the dress, and Jenny was soon back in her own clothes. Florence wanted to begin work on it immediately, determined to have it ready for the next day just as she'd promised.

"Is it all right to pay for it when I come to collect it?" Jenny asked and looked as if she fully expected Florence to say no.

"Of course, it is," Florence said, deciding to give her the benefit of the doubt.

"It's just that I'll have my husband with me tomorrow, and he'll be the one paying for it," Jenny went on, and Florence smiled.

"You're married?" How young she was, and yet many girls of their class married at sixteen.

"Yes!" Jenny said gruffly. "Why? Didn't you think anyone would marry me?"

"I didn't think anything of the sort, Jenny. I'm pleased for you, that's all."

"Oh, well..." Jenny said, entirely wrongfooted by the idea that anybody in Limehouse could just be simply pleased for another, no hint of jealousy, no hint of cynicism, no spiteful remarks. "Well, thank you," she said, somewhat shyly.

"I'll have it ready for you tomorrow. Come in whatever time you like," Florence said and smiled again, strangely relieved when Jenny made her way out of the shop.

It has been a peculiarly exhausting encounter. Jenny

had reminded her of old feelings she would sooner forget. The days when she and Queenie had been struggling. The days when her every working moment at the mill had been made a misery by the young woman whom she had just sold a dress to. Florence didn't want to hold onto those feelings. A part of her wanted to cling to her grudge, remembering Jenny's glee when Florence had been thrown out of the mill. But if she held onto the grudge, she would have to hold on to the old feelings of despair, and she had no intention of doing that. Life was good now, and that was all Florence wanted to feel.

However, not very many more hours passed that day before Florence was once again reminded of the past. She had decided to close up a little early since the alterations to Jenny's dress had already been made, and she had a rabbit that she wanted to make a good and hearty stew from. Dear Winnie would have prepared the vegetables, she had no doubt about it, but the rabbit would take a little cooking, and she wanted to make sure her dear old friend ate well before bedtime.

With that in mind, Florence closed the door firmly and secured the bolts, and she was about to pull down the shutters when her eye was drawn a little further up the street.

It was early spring, and the nights were getting mercifully shorter. The sun had gone down, more or less, but it wasn't yet dark. Florence, close enough to the glass that her breath fogged its surface, was watching a man staggering along the street. It wasn't an unusual sight in Limehouse, but there was something familiar about the man, something which made it impossible for Florence to stop watching.

It was then that she realised it was Jimmy Bates. How different he looked! She'd seen him regularly in the beginning, when she had first moved into the little room at the back of Winnie's shop. He'd tried to intimidate her from afar, glaring at her from across the street, but noticeably never daring to approach the door for fear that the deceptively tough old Winnie Gibbons might go at him with a broom.

After some months, however, he seemed to have tired of the whole thing, and it must have been a year and a half since she had last set eyes on him.

Florence wanted to watch dispassionately, but she couldn't. Queenie had been right, always, when she said that Florence was just too kind and just too sensitive. It was clear that Jimmy Bates was full of drink, and clearer still from his appearance that it wasn't a one-off. It was too early in the day for this to be a simple case of one too many at the Rose and Crown. She'd been in Limehouse for long enough now to know a drunk when she saw one.

As hateful as he'd been, Florence couldn't help but wonder what had happened to him. He was a little stooped now, and he looked very much older than what must surely only have been his twenty years. Putting everything else to one side, she couldn't help but think what a shame it was that a young and handsome man could be so changed by too much strong liquor. Gin, more than likely.

Florence drew in her breath when he stumbled and dropped to his knees and had been about to draw back the bolts and run out to help him when Queenie's voice filled her mind. *Don't ever trust that man, no matter what*. That's what Queenie would have said.

Florence's hand hovered over the bolts for a moment as she watched Jimmy get to his feet. As he continued on his way, she determinedly pulled down the shutter at last and decided that she would think no more about it. She didn't wish him any harm, despite everything, but she knew it would be unwise to do anything that might invite him into her life once again.

lorence had never realised that there was a solicitor's office in Limehouse until she received a letter asking her to attend. It was just a week after Winnie's funeral, and the letter declared that her presence was required for the reading of the last will and testament of Winnie Gibbons.

Florence had kept the shop closed since Winnie had died, a mark of respect for the woman who had, in a very real sense, saved Florence's life. It was some small comfort to Florence that, this time, she had enough resources that she might give proper time to her own grieving, unlike when her grandma had died.

She didn't really know what she was going to do next, and she sincerely hoped that the solicitor would be able to furnish her with the details of the landlord of the property so that she might be the one to pay the rent now. She didn't want to leave the shop, even though she didn't feel much better about Limehouse now than ever she did. But the shop felt like home, and this time she didn't want to leave. She wanted to be surrounded by her memories of Winnie, of the two of them sitting at the table sewing chattering, of the ease she was able to bring Winnie in her later years by making a success of the place.

"Ah, Miss Goodyear, I presume?" A tall and well-dressed man in his middle fifties strode towards her, his hand outstretched, as she cautiously made her way into the offices of Merton, Merton, and Pirbright. "I'm Wilberforce Pirbright, my dear," he went on, by way of introduction.

"It's nice to meet you, Mr Pirbright," Florence said shyly.

"Well, do come into my office, Miss Goodyear, we have much to go through." He held out an arm and she followed it in the general direction of his office. "You are, of course, the only attendee today. I'm sure it will come as no surprise to you that Mrs Gibbons has made everything over to you."

"She was with a very kind lady," Florence said, not imagining that poor Winnie had a great deal to give her. Nonetheless, every little would help if she were to have any chance of keeping the shop on.

Florence settled down in a deceptively comfortable chair set at the desk opposite Mr Pirbright. He took his own seat and retrieved an amusing looking pair of pince-nez from his pocket, perching them on the end of his nose. It made Florence smile, for she knew that Winnie, a woman who always wore proper spectacles with arms, would have been greatly amused to see so fine a gentleman wearing the cheap, armless vision aids.

"Now, I have Mrs Gibbons' last will and testament here, but perhaps you would prefer me to simply give you a summary of what's inside?"

"Yes, thank you," Florence said, feeling a little out of her depth. She'd never spoken to a solicitor in her life, much less been inside a solicitor's office.

"As I mentioned before, Mrs Gibbons has left her entire estate to you," he went on, and Florence thought that Winnie would have been similarly amused to hear her worldly possessions described as *an estate.* "Which includes, broadly, the building housing the shop and the living accommodation above, all stock currently contained within, and all of the personal possessions Mrs Gibbons leaves behind, which I believe are entirely contained within the room above the shop."

"The building?" Florence said, thinking that he'd surely made a mistake. "Forgive me, sir, but I don't know who the building belongs to. To be honest, I had very much hoped that you would be able to tell me the name of the landlord so that I might contact him and ask if I could be considered to take over the tenancy. I would like to stay in the shop, you see, and continue to run it."

"The landlord?" And now it was Mr Pirbright's turn to look confused. "What landlord, my dear?"

"The landlord, Mr Pirbright," Florence said. "The person who owns the building that Mrs Gibbons rented."

"But Mrs Gibbons didn't rent the building, my dear.

She wasn't the tenant, Miss Goodyear, she was the owner."

"Mrs Gibbons owned the building?" Florence asked, her mouth dropping open. "But are you quite sure, Mr Pirbright?"

"I am in a line of business, Miss Goodyear, which requires me to be sure," he said and boomed with laughter. "I can promise you faithfully, Miss Goodyear, that Mrs Gibbons was the sole owner of the building at 58 West Street in Limehouse. The building was purchased by her husband several decades ago, before his own demise, and naturally, since Mr and Mrs Gibbons had no children, nor any other relatives, the whole thing went to Mrs Gibbons when her husband passed."

"I see," Florence said, her heart pounding. "You must think me very silly, Mr Pirbright, but these were things that Mrs Gibbons and I never discussed. We never talked about money and that sort of thing, not really."

"And with good reason. Mrs Gibbons doesn't leave a great deal of money, it's true. She has two-hundred-and-twenty-seven pounds in an account which, I believe, is takings from the shop built up over a number of years."

"Goodness," Florence said, thinking that her idea of a great deal of money and Mr Pirbright's varied wildly. As far as she was aware, beyond the Daventrys, Florence had never known a person who owned two-hundred-and-twenty-seven pounds.

"So, that is the building at 58 West Street in Limehouse, its entire contents in both the shop and the room above, and the two-hundred-and-twenty-seven pounds in the bank. Now then, I shall need the details of your own bank so that I might have the money transferred there, of course."

"Mr Pirbright, I have never had a bank account in my life," Florence said and fought an instinct to laugh.

"Not to worry, I shall help you deal with that. Now then, you are at least eighteen years old, are you not?"

"I am." Florence nodded. "I am exactly eighteen years and six months."

"And is your father living?"

"No," Florence said, deciding not to tell this fine and

educated man that she had no idea who her father was.

"Then I shall be able to open an account for you in your own right unless you have another guardian?"

"Not since Mrs Gibbon passed, no," Florence said sadly.

"Then you are a free agent, and I shouldn't have too much difficulty in arranging an account for you. There will, of course, be a small fee for my services."

"Of course," Florence said, and hoped that the small fee did not amount to exactly two-hundred-and-twenty-seven pounds.

"I shall let you take a little time to read through the will," he said, pushing it across the desk. "And there is also a letter here for you, written by Mrs Gibbons herself some weeks before her passing. I daresay you would be pleased for a little privacy in which to read it, so I shall leave you be and have my assistant bring you in some tea." He was already on his feet.

"Thank you," she said, staring at the envelope on the desk with her name on it, written in Winnie's familiar hand.

As soon as Mr Pirbright left the room, Florence immediately opened the envelope. She would leave the will for now, for she was certain it could tell her no more than Mr Pirbright had told her already in terms of what she could expect. But the letter was something else altogether, her last conversation with the woman she had come to love like a grandmother.

My Dearest Florence,

I do hope you're managing without me. I hope you're not too sad, I was a very old lady, you know. And I shall be perfectly all right, safe in heaven with my dear Wilf. I hope he hasn't changed too much since I last saw him, excepting my hope that he has picked up a few more practical skills and some better conversation in the meantime.

But it is not myself I worry for, but you, Florence. You made the last years of my life so happy. I had imagined that I would spend those years in the same loneliness as had existed before, but that wasn't so, and I'm eternally grateful for it.

It is my dearest wish that you stay in the shop, that you continue to make such a wonderful success of it. I know you will do well there, continuing to build upon the wonderful work that you have done already. And I should like you to consider the room above the shop as your own now, moving out of that tiny place on the ground floor, and treating the upstairs as your sanctuary. Make it nice, my dear. Make it pretty. Use some of that money that I have left in the bank for you.

Finally, it would do my heart good to think that you might find yourself in a position to open your heart one day to a nice young man. I have known ever since I met you that your heart belonged to your dear Marcus Daventry, but I shouldn't like to see you alone forever on account of it. If you cannot have him, then find yourself someone as good, or almost as good. Don't wander through the world alone, there isn't much happiness in it.

Now all that is left for me to do is join your dear grandmother in her determination to watch over you for the rest of your life. And you may be certain that I will do it, for I am most determined. And so, goodnight, my dear girl, and thank you for making this old woman's last year's such happy ones.

Oh yes, and if that Jimmy Bates comes a-calling, you know where the broom is.

With all my love,

Winnie.

As she finished, and with tears streaming down her face, Mr Pirbright's assistant crept into the room with a tray of tea. She smiled warmly and kindly, clearly used to emotional clients sitting at Mr Pirbright's desk.

"Your tea, Miss Goodyear," the woman said and smiled again before leaving Florence to read Winnie's beautiful letter one more time.

Although Florence had been safe and content in her shop, the weeks since Winnie had died had been lonely ones. She'd busied herself doing just as Winnie had suggested, changing things in that little room upstairs to her own liking. It was her new little nest now that she had no need to sleep in the back room of the shop any longer.

Business continued to boom, largely because Florence found herself at such a loose end without

Winnie to take care of that she spent long hours making dresses, filling the shop and drawing working-class women from all around. The truth was, she was even beginning to draw a lower-middle-class woman or two who was looking for a well-made everyday dress, the price tag of which her husband would not baulk at.

Since women made up the greater part of the footfall in her shop every day, Florence was surprised when a tall, well-dressed man let himself in one bright and sunny afternoon. He seemed a little awkward, a little cautious, and yet Florence thought he was the sort of man who ought to be brimming with confidence.

He was clearly a gentleman, well-dressed and tall, and very handsome with his dark hair and bright blue eyes. And they were bright, bright blue.

Florence's mouth fell open. He was older, broader, with no hint of the boy he had once been, but the man standing in her shop studying her as closely as she was studying him was, without question, Marcus Daventry.

"Marcus?" she said, her voice no more than a whisper.

"I've looked all over for you, Florence. I had begun to think that you must have left Limehouse altogether."

"No, I never left. I wanted to, but I never did," Florence said, her eyes filling with tears that even speedy blinking could not dispel. "I can't believe you're here."

"I can't believe I'm here either. I thought that this was going to be just another dead end, another red herring."

"What do you mean?" Her hands were shaking, and she put down her needle and thread and rose slowly from the table.

"I searched and searched for you, Florence. I've asked questions, I've bought dubious looking characters drinks in some of the worst pubs I've ever seen, and all to no avail. In fact, I am bound to say that the people of Limehouse are neither friendly nor helpful."

"No, they are neither friendly nor helpful," Florence said, the tears rolling down her cheeks now.

"So, as always, you are the brightest point for miles around." He took a few steps towards her and

Florence, unable to stop herself, she ran into his arms. "It really is good to see you, Florence."

"And it is good to see you," Florence said, almost unintelligible for her sobs.

"How did you end up here? I never imagined you in a shop."

"It's my shop, Marcus," Florence said, unable to hold back her pride, even in her wonderful state of shock.

"Well, good for you. Good for you, Florence Smith," he said, and Florence felt a sharp pang of fear. Of course, her beloved Marcus didn't know who she really was. He didn't know that she was Florence Goodyear, the daughter of a prostitute.

"And what about you? Are you back in London again?" Florence asked, not wanting to dwell too much on her own circumstances, not until she'd had a chance to think about how she would go about telling him the truth of it all. Because, in the end, she knew she must one day tell him the truth.

"I'm working in London, Florence, although I still live in my parents' house in Bedfordshire."

"That seems like a very long way to go to work," Florence said humorously, and Marcus laughed.

"I spend Tuesday, Wednesday, and Thursday night in rooms not too far from the office."

"The office?"

"Yes, Cooper and Soames," he said, pausing for her reaction.

"Cooper and Soames? But isn't that...?"

"The very same, but that is a long story. A story for another day, I think. That is if you would consent to set eyes on me again?" It was a question, and he released her for long enough to raise his eyebrows. "Well? Can I come back?"

"Of course, you can come back, Marcus. You can come back anytime you choose," Florence said and felt lightheaded with joy, excitement, and fear.

"Oh, I am pleased. I cannot tell you how much I've missed you and Queenie." He peered around Florence towards the back of the shop. "Where is she, by the way? I want to see if she's as feisty as she used to be."

"Oh, Marcus," Florence said and bit her bottom lip. "She's gone, she's gone."

"When?" Marcus asked, and Florence felt her heart almost burst when she saw his beautiful blue eyes fill with tears.

"Just six months after we left you. It was her lungs, in the end."

"I'm so sorry, Florence. I'm so sorry that everything went wrong, and you had to manage that all alone.

"I know. I know." And she leaned against him once more, finding the most wonderful refuge in his arms.

CHAPTER SIXTEEN

*M*arcus visited, without fail, three times a week. He had lodgings in Farringdon, not far from the city offices of Cooper and Soames, and he made a point of taking a brougham carriage every evening to spend an hour in Limehouse with Florence.

They had been as at ease with each other as they had always been, and yet Florence could feel that they each had something held back. They each had something to tell, and she was certain that neither one of them were yet ready to tell it. Certainly, Florence wasn't ready to start filling in all the details Marcus had missed in the last five years. She was certain that it would be the end of this wonderful reunion, and she wanted to make it last just a little while longer. Whatever time Florence had with Marcus now, she knew it would have to last her a lifetime.

"You seem a hundred miles away, where are you?" Marcus asked as the two of them sat in the backroom of the shop taking tea.

Since she had moved upstairs into Winnie's room, Florence had rearranged the little room at the back of the shop which had once been her nest. It served as a storeroom for her fabrics, with a pretty little table and chairs that she had picked up at the flea market. It was where she took her breaks, always bringing a tray of tea down from upstairs to enjoy mid-morning.

She'd never invited Marcus into the room upstairs. It was as if she wanted him to know that she was a decent young woman with firm morals, almost setting the scene for the day when she would have to tell him the truth of her origins. She always brought a tray of tea down for them, and he'd never made any mention of wanting to see the room she lived in. How different he was from the likes of Jimmy Bates.

"I'm right here, I promise," Florence said and laughed. "I've had a busy day."

"Is that a good thing or a bad thing?"

"It is both," Florence said, grinning at him.

"You always were too clever for me, weren't you?" He smiled, that wonderful handsome smile, his bright blue eyes narrowing, the skin around them wrinkling as that smile reached his eyes. They were the finest eyes in all the world.

"No, I don't think I was ever too clever for you, Marcus. A good match, perhaps?"

"You've learnt to be a politician in the time we've been parted," Marcus said and continued to laugh.

"A dressmaker has to be a politician," Florence began. "Especially when somebody wants to leave the shop wearing something that doesn't suit them at all."

"I imagine many an awkward conversation has taken place under this roof."

"Yes, and perhaps a great many more to come,"

Florence said, thinking of her own situation and feeling that familiar worry.

"What is it?" he asked.

"Nothing, nothing at all."

"I know you. I might not have seen you over the last few years, but I still know you."

"It's nothing to worry about."

"I do wish you would trust me. I wonder sometimes if you blame me for what happened all those years ago. For my father, for Wimbledon. For your losses, and how you had to deal with them alone."

"Oh Marcus, why on earth would I blame you?"

"Because I didn't come to help. I didn't come to find you back then."

"No, no, you were barely seventeen years old and you had troubles enough in your own family. I was not the only one who lost things, who was suffering. I know you suffered too."

"Yes, but I suffered in leafy Ampthill, not hideous Limehouse."

"It's not a competition, Marcus. Loss is loss, no matter your surroundings."

"You still have that wonderful ability to get to the very heart of things, to reduce it to a single sentence that makes absolute sense."

"There, now I have two talents. Dressmaking and sense-making."

"And humour. Let's not forget that wit of yours."

"Living here in Limehouse these last years, a person becomes more used to insults and spite than compliments and kindness. There are only so many compliments I can reasonably accept in a day without turning to dust."

"Then I shall hold back my compliments for Friday."

"Friday?" she said with confusion. "You generally return home to Bedfordshire after work on Friday."

"And I will be this Friday. But I'm not talking about the evening, I'm talking about the daytime. You see, I have it in mind to take the day off work on Friday, and if you could do the same, I thought we could perhaps take a little trip to Wimbledon Common. The weather's been fine all week, and I don't expect

Friday will be any different. We could take a little picnic on the Common, couldn't we?"

"Oh, that would be lovely," Florence said, closing her eyes and trying to draw to mind images of the wonderful park she hadn't seen for five years.

"Have you been back?" he asked, seeming a little serious now.

"To Wimbledon? No, I haven't seen it since the day I left."

"No, neither have I."

"Are you sure Wimbledon Common is where you want to go on Friday? It won't be too hard?"

"I'm sure. I think I want us both to be back in the place where we were once so happy. Perhaps it would be a starting point, a way for us both to be happy again."

"Then Wimbledon Common it is," Florence said, and as Marcus began to get to his feet, she felt that familiar sense of mild bereavement. It was getting late and it was time for him to go back to his rooms in Farringdon.

"I shan't see you tomorrow evening, Florence. I have some work I'll need to finish at Cooper and Soames if I'm to take Friday to myself. But I shall be here bright and early Friday morning to collect you."

"And I will be ready."

Florence walked him through the shop and reached out to slide the bolts back on the door. Marcus was smiling at her, looking into her face, Florence held her breath. She was so certain that he was about to kiss her that she was already blushing. He leaned forward, and then gently kissed her cheek. It was like falling through a tunnel into the past, remembering that day when he had kissed her cheek and it had almost broken her heart. She had assumed it meant that he didn't love her, that he only thought of her as a sister or a friend. She was beginning to realise that she'd been wrong. He'd just been a boy of seventeen who no more knew what to do back then than she did.

"Until Friday," Marcus said in a low voice.

"Until Friday."

And then, without warning, he leaned forward again and gently kissed her lips. It was brief, so brief she wondered later if it had even happened at all. And yet, despite the brevity, the feel of his lips on hers created a memory that Florence knew she would never forget.

M arcus walked away from the shop with something of a spring in his step. As always, the brougham driver had waited for him at the top of the street, glad for a few extra coins to do no more than sit there and enjoy the cool evening air.

His decision to kiss her, really kiss her, seemed to have been made without his knowledge. He'd kissed her lips before he'd known he was going to, and he was just relieved that she seemed to be pleased about it. Well, not repulsed, at any rate.

Marcus could feel something changing in his world, and he had the greatest hopes now. Greater hopes than he'd ever had before. He wished that he had made his move sooner, that he had looked for her long before now. But he knew that he couldn't have done that, the time hadn't been right. He'd had things of his own to get to the bottom of, things which had to be put right to some degree before he could find her.

But now he had everything in place; he had a good job with his father's old firm, despite the difficulties, and had a future ahead of him now. It was a future that he had never believed possible just twelve months before, so how could he have found her then? How could he have looked for her, declared his love for her at last, and then told her he had no way to take care of her? Now he did. Now the future looked bright and their trip to Wimbledon Common even brighter.

"Looking pleased with yourself, sir," a man stepped out in front of him, and Marcus, shaken out of his daydream, stared at him in surprise.

"I beg your pardon?" Marcus said, assuming the man was about to make an attempt to relieve him of his possessions. Marcus stood his ground; he wouldn't be mugged by anybody.

"So, she's found herself a fine gentleman, at last, has she?" The man's voice was a lot younger than his face, and Marcus realised that there probably wasn't much to choose between their ages. The strong smell of alcohol immediately gave away the reason for the man's prematurely aged face.

"What on earth are you talking about?" Marcus said, losing patience. Surely it would be quicker and quieter if the man just attempted to mug him and they could get on with things.

"Miss hoity-toity in there!" the man said, inclining his dark head towards Florence's shop. "Don't be fooled, she's not as posh as she seems. Got a nasty past, that one."

"I sincerely hope you're not talking about Florence Smith, my dear fellow. If you are, then you are going to need to take that back, otherwise, you are going to find yourself on the wrong end of my temper."

"No need for that, sir, I'm only trying to help you." The man, almost as tall as Marcus, looked nowhere near as fit and healthy and likely not in any position to win a physical argument.

"Just get to the point," Marcus said with some exasperation.

"She hasn't always been doing so well for herself. Fell on hard times she did, back when she and that old grandma of hers first came here. Then, of course, the old bird died, and your girl there didn't have a penny to her name. Well, not until she came to work for me."

"What do you mean?" Marcus asked, his fists clenched at his sides, his heart pounding uncomfortably.

"I think you know what I mean," the man said with a lascivious smile. "It's the oldest profession in the world, isn't it?"

"I don't believe you. I don't know what it is you want, but you're not going to get it." Marcus was furious.

"I don't want anything. I don't want money, I don't want work, I don't want anything at all from you. All I wanted to do was help, nothing more. I don't expect you to believe me, but you know what the old saying is, don't you? Like mother, like daughter." The man was being cryptic and enjoying it.

"Florence Smith's mother died in childbirth. You're talking about a woman she's never known, so I politely suggest that you have the wrong person." Marcus felt a heavy feeling in his gut.

"If you don't believe me, then believe the public records office. That girl's mother was a prostitute just the same. She was a prostitute who was murdered, you'll find the information if you care to look for it. But don't go looking for any Smiths, there ain't no Florence Smith, nor Gladys Smith. Try Goodyear." The man gave a final sneer of triumph before turning to walk away.

Marcus looked back to the shop, but the shutter was down, and Florence was probably already upstairs in her room. He couldn't go back; he couldn't just stand there and ask her about it, could he?

He headed along the street, keen to be sitting in the brougham alone with his thoughts. He couldn't believe that Florence had ever worked for that awful man, but what did he know? As much as he thought he'd suffered, what did he know of the true suffering of those who lived in poverty in places like Limehouse? As the driver urged the horse away and the brougham began to speed through the night, Marcus closed his eyes and wondered what on earth he should do next.

CHAPTER SEVENTEEN

*I*n the end, Florence decided to open the shop. She'd waited for four hours for Marcus to appear, spending most of those hours standing by the door, peering out through the shutters to see if the man she loved was approaching.

As the morning turned into afternoon, she had to admit to herself that their planned trip to Wimbledon common wasn't going to happen that day. Perhaps it wasn't going to happen any day.

She tried not to allow such fatalistic thoughts, but she couldn't help worrying. Of course, there was every chance that something had happened at Cooper and Soames, that they couldn't spare him for the day. Yes, that's probably what it was. But wouldn't he have found some way to get a message to her? He'd have paid a boy a few coins to run to Limehouse with a note. That's who Marcus was. That's who she knew him to be; a thoughtful boy who had turned into a thoughtful man.

With nothing else to do, she lifted the shutters and opened the door, letting it be known to any passing trade that her shop was, after all, open for business that day. Trying to keep herself busy, Florence began to attend to some of the alterations that were due to be ready the following week. But if she'd hoped it would keep her mind off it, it didn't. In the end, she threw the sewing back down on the table with a sigh and leaned back in her chair. She almost screamed when she saw Jimmy Bates standing there in front of her. Florence had been so absorbed by her worries that she hadn't heard him creep in through the open door, as silent and as sneaky as a cat.

"Jimmy, for heaven's sake!" Florence said, her pounding heart making her angry. "You almost scared me to death."

"Well, we wouldn't want that, would we?" He was slurring his words, and Florence realised, with some concern, that he was drunk.

It had been a long time since she'd seen him, and his condition seemed to have deteriorated much further than she had witnessed that day when she had spied on him from the window. No longer was he that proud, upright, cocky young man. He looked old and miserable, finally realising that the gin, or whatever was his poison, had taken such a hold of him that he couldn't function in the world the way he had once done. As afraid as she was, she realised that she felt sad too.

"What do you want?" Florence asked, trying to make her voice sound kind and reasonable. She didn't want him to know that she was afraid; the Jimmy Bates she knew thrived on such things.

"I just wanted to let you know that you might not be seeing that young man of yours again," he slurred, and Florence was on her feet in an instant.

"Why? What have you done to him?" She felt pain and fury surging through her veins. "If you've hurt him, Jimmy Bates, if you've done something to him, so help me God I will rip your guts out!" She was snarling, coming around the table ready to claw the eyeballs from his skull. She had never felt like this before, and it was a terrible thing. It controlled her;

there was no hint of the Florence she ordinarily was to be found anywhere inside her.

"Calm yourself," Jimmy said, sensing her fury even in his drunken state. He backed away a little, holding his hands out in front of him. How the tables were turned! If he had hurt Marcus, Florence felt certain that she would kill him. "He isn't harmed, he's just not coming back. I'm afraid I had a word with him, you see," Jimmy went on, still backing away, but smirking now.

"You did what?" Florence couldn't calm herself; she couldn't get hold of that fury.

"I thought the man had a right to know who he was getting himself tangled up with, that's all. A fine gentleman can't be consorting with a lady of the night after all, can he?"

"But I'm not..." Florence said, scowling at him until her eyes burned.

"Oh yes, that's right, you never did take me up on that job offer, did you?" he said and made a performance of tapping his forehead. "Whoops-a-daisy looks like I might have given that man of yours the wrong impression. Still, he'll believe it right enough when he does his own asking about and learns that Florence Smith is really Florence Goodyear, daughter of the prostitute, Gladys Goodyear, who was strangled to death." He began to laugh, an evil, self-satisfied noise. If only he had laughed that way the first day she'd met him. If only he hadn't seemed so pleasant, so guileless. If only Florence had never stopped to speak to him.

After all these years, after all his trying, Jimmy Bates had finally found a way to ruin Florence's life. He'd taken Marcus from her, he'd taken the one good thing left in her world. The fury wouldn't die down, and finally, Florence flew at him, clawing at his face, kicking his shins. He moved backwards out the shop and into the street, and finally, Florence stopped clawing at him, drew her arm back, and punched him square on the jaw.

She had no idea that she ever possessed such strength, and clearly, Jimmy Bates hadn't either, for he fell backwards, landing hard on his backside for all to see. There were plenty on the street, many of whom didn't think much of him. A cheer went up, and some even clapped, and Florence stood there over him, glaring down, enjoying the humiliation that this spiteful man so richly deserved.

She went back into the shop, leaving him sitting there in the dust. She closed the door, threw across the bolts, and pulled down the shutters.

Now that the fury was abating, Florence felt horribly sick.

When the gin ran out, Jimmy picked up the empty bottle and hurled it at the wall of the alleyway. He didn't have a penny in his pocket to get more, and no girl in his power whom he could send out to earn him a little money. That was all gone now, and as he leaned against the cold brick wall, he tried to work out why.

He stared at the shards of glass, the dim glow of the streetlamps reflecting in the jagged pieces. The drink had taken him, he knew that he just didn't know when or why. He'd always liked a drop, he'd always enjoyed that sense of letting go with his cronies in the Rose and Crown, the good old days when he'd had girls aplenty and pockets full of money. The drink had crept up on him, it had inserted itself into his life slowly, quietly, until one day he woke up and realised that it had taken him altogether. He was in its grip, and he couldn't escape.

Feeling sorry for himself, Jimmy searched for somebody to blame. There must be somebody to blame, somebody who had driven him to this dark place and stolen everything from his life. Everybody was always stealing, taking things, from the moment his father had been stolen from him.

Jimmy sat up a little straighter; yes, that was right. His father had been stolen from him, and everything had been slipping away ever since. Even though he thought he'd escaped it, that he was riding high, the loss was waiting for him around the next corner. And why? Why was that? He nodded his head slowly. It was her. If she'd never come to Limehouse, if she'd stayed away, living her anonymous life in Wimbledon, Jimmy would never have been so painfully reminded of the day he had watched his father hanging from a rope. His old man's head swathed in the hessian sack, his feet kicking as everybody laughed and jeered and said what a fine jig he was doing.

Florence had brought all of that back, and with it, she had pushed him slowly but surely towards the bottle. It was the only explanation he could find, and it sat well with him. It gave him a sense of being right, of being the victim, of wanting revenge.

He tipped his head back and stared up at the moon, trying to fight off the old images of his father hanging, of the baying crowd. But as soon as he had rid himself of that image, it was replaced by another. Of himself, the once proud and cocky young man who thought he had all of Limehouse at his feet. But now he sat in the dust, floored by a little girl, nursing his wounds as the same old crowd had cheered and clapped.

It was her. She was to blame for all of it, and she would pay.

Filled with a sudden sense of purpose, Jimmy got to his feet. He was going to put an end to this, all of it. He was going to be rid of her at last, for only when she was gone could he return to his former glory.

F lorence had slept fitfully, having only a few minutes' sleep at a time before she was wide awake again. Ever since Jimmy had told her what he'd done, she'd tried to work out what she should do for the best. If only she'd told Marcus before. If only she hadn't waited for so long, trying to lengthen the time she had left with him. If she had just had a little more courage, if she had just been honest, there was the slimmest chance that Marcus might've understood and still kissed her anyway.

But now, how would he ever trust her again? How could she even speak to him now that he undoubtedly believed that she had worked for Jimmy Bates in the same profession that had taken her mother's life so many years before? She could protest until she was blue in the face, why should he believe her?

Florence drifted off again, so exhausted that sleep was determined to have her, if only for a little while. But when she awoke again in the darkness, it was something other than Marcus this time which had prodded her into consciousness. It was a smell.

Florence sat up in her bed and blinked furiously,

trying to let her eyes adjust to the pale moonlight coming in through the window. She drew in a deep breath, trying, in her sleepy state, to identify the aroma. When she finally realised it was smoke, her heart began to pound. She flew out of bed and ran for the door, but when she opened it, the billowing smoke waiting outside drifted in to overwhelm her. She slammed the door closed again, the hot smoke in her throat, in her lungs, making her cough so violently that she suddenly thought of Queenie. Queenie had coughed like this; Queenie had died like this.

Was she to die too? Was it time for her to join her mother and grandmother at last? But she didn't want to. Florence wanted to survive, and so she hurried across to the sash window and slid the bottom panel up as high as it would go. She looked down, and it suddenly felt so very high. Even the low buildings of Limehouse were high when a person needed to jump.

She could hear shouts outside now; no doubt everybody could see that the shop was on fire, that the whole building would soon be taken. The shouts were at the front, and her window was at the back. Feeling a dreadful sense of panic, a horrible, sickening fear, Florence screamed and screamed out of the window, praying that somebody at the front would hear her.

Her throat was raw from the smoke and from the screaming, and she had just come to the conclusion that she would, in the end, have to jump, when she realised that there were people below. She looked down and could see men, men she didn't recognise, labouring between them to rest a long ladder against the wall, all the way up to her window.

Florence turned, hurriedly putting on her boots and searching the darkness, the smoky room, for her dress. She didn't want to be left with nothing but a nightgown, and she risked two minutes more in that awful environment to at least be dressed.

She finally climbed down the ladder to safety, and just minutes later, the flames lit up the window above. Realising then just how close she'd been to death, Florence gave in and lost consciousness, falling into the arms of one of the men who had rescued her.

CHAPTER EIGHTEEN

he timbers of the building were still smouldering the next morning, and Florence stood on the street staring at the devastation. Everything was gone. Her fabric, the dresses she had worked so hard to make, everything. The floor had given way, and her burnt little bed rested awkwardly on the debris, the mattress almost gone, nothing left but the iron springs beneath.

She was alone, even though there were plenty who walked past to have a good look at her misfortune. The people of Limehouse might have been good enough to save her life, but they weren't so good that they couldn't enjoy the spectacle.

Realising that she had nothing left, not a person, not

a home, nothing but the clothes she stood up in, Florence wondered if she really should have climbed out of that window at all. She knew already that it was Jimmy Bates, she didn't need anybody to confirm that. The policeman told her, of course, but she had just looked at him blankly when he said that a little boy had seen Jimmy stealing paraffin from the Rose and Crown in the dead of night, and one of the local drunks had seen him running away from the shop, the bright flames already consuming everything in sight.

"He'll go to prison for it, you can be pleased about that," the young policeman said, as Florence mutely continued to stare at him. "Well, it looks like you'll have to find somewhere else to live now," he went on, his advice seeming pointless to a woman who had nothing and nobody.

When the policeman left, Florence turned to stare at the shop once again. This life was full of loss, but this life was the only thing that had been left to her. She'd lost Wimbledon and Marcus, then Queenie, she'd lost her job at the mill, she'd lost the room that she shared with her grandmother. She'd lost Winnie, and then she'd lost the shop. And finally, she'd lost Marcus, *again*.

"Florence?" The voice behind her startled her, and she spun around to see Marcus, his bright blue eyes wide and shocked. "My God, what happened?"

"It was done on purpose, Marcus," Florence said, exhausted, bereft, and confused as to Marcus's sudden presence. She felt as if she were wading through a dream that she couldn't wake up from, nothing seemed real. "Jimmy Bates."

"Bates?" he said, a look of recognition. "Any connection to Warren Bates?"

"His son. He's been trying to destroy me for a long time, and now he has. He's taken everything. He's taken my livelihood, my home, and you."

"He might have taken the first two, but he certainly hasn't taken me. I assume this Jimmy Bates is the one who caught up with me to tell me his tale, is he? He failed to mention that the man who murdered your mother was his own father."

"The very same. He came to me yesterday gloating, telling me that you were never coming back. But not everything he told you was true, Marcus, although I doubt you'll believe me now."

"If you think I believed you had ever worked with him, I didn't."

"I thought you must have. I thought that's why you didn't come yesterday."

"Ah, I am sorry about that. It's why I'm here so early today, to beg for your forgiveness," he said and smiled at her. "You see, I did want to know. I wanted to know what you'd suffered, because I realised, finally, that you were never going to tell me. But I needed to know. I needed to know what you'd suffered. And so, I decided to go to the public records office, just as that little runt suggested. I found the details of your mother's death, and I really am so sorry."

"I never knew. Grandma always hid it from me."

"With the best of intentions, I'm sure."

"And now I have nothing. Jimmy Bates will go to prison, but how does that help me?"

"I'm here," Marcus said, reaching out to wipe away some soot from her cheek.

"Even though you know my background? Even though I didn't tell you?"

"You once told me, many years ago, that a real friend remains a friend no matter what has happened. Well, I'm here to tell you the same thing."

"You don't despise me?"

"You are the strongest, bravest, most beautiful woman I've ever met. I've only ever loved you; I could never despise you."

"And I've only ever loved you too. That's why I found it so hard to tell you the truth. I didn't want this to end. I needed more time, more time to be with you before I lost you again."

"You're not the only one who held something back. I held something back myself for the very same reason."

"What?"

"It was my father's fault," he said, and his blue eyes narrowed. "Back in Wimbledon, losing everything, it was him. He really did give away inside information to another firm, and he did it for money. I wanted to tell you, but I suppose I was still a little ashamed."

"I'm so sorry."

"I've dealt with the shame of it for so long, but he told us the truth in the end. He was ashamed too, ashamed that a moment of weakness had lost us everything. But that truth rather set me free, it made me let go of the guilt that I was holding for suspecting him for so long."

"Your poor father."

"Only you could be so understanding, Florence."

"But you work for Cooper and Soames? How did you manage that?"

"I went to them and told them who I was. I didn't try to hide anything, and I made it clear that I knew exactly what my father had done. I wasn't really expecting anything, but they surprised me. They liked my honesty, and they hoped that I would be as good with trading stocks as my father had been. For all his faults, he was second to none in that world."

"So, what do we do with our truth now, Marcus?"

"How about a new shop?" Marcus said and grinned. "But not here in Limehouse, Florence. I think you've probably had enough of this place by now, haven't you?"

"I don't think I have enough to begin again," she said and looked down at herself. "Given that what you see me wearing is all I possess."

"I have the means now to look after you. I have my own world and my own means. I'm finally fit to take care of you."

"What do you think I should call the shop? Smith's or Goodyear's?" she said, bringing that final lie into the conversation.

"I think you should call it Daventry's. After all, I'm rather hoping that you will be a married woman by then."

"Oh Marcus, after everything, do you really mean that?"

"I've only ever loved you, Florence, and I will only ever love you. What point is a life of means when you can't share it with the only person you will ever love?"

"And I've only ever loved you, Marcus. It broke my heart to leave Wimbledon behind. I've never been happier than I was there when I was with you."

"Then let's go back, Florence. Let's be married and let's go back to Wimbledon."

"Marcus, I do love you," Florence said, tears of happiness streaming down her face as she flung her arms around his neck.

EPILOGUE

"*I*'ll have the alterations done for you by Friday, Mrs Price-Martin." Florence smiled, and the woman nodded. Another satisfied customer.

"Are you sure you're going to have it done by Friday?" Marcus asked, appearing from the back of the shop the moment he heard the door close on Mrs Price-Martin. "You already have so much to do."

"I'll manage perfectly. I do enjoy Saturdays, Marcus." Florence turned to smile at her husband.

"Why Saturdays?"

"Because you're not working at Cooper and Soames, and you always spend Saturday here with me in the shop."

"I know I'm not much help, but I do like to keep you company."

"And you keep me company admirably."

"Sooner or later, you really are going to have to get a little help in this place. You're so popular with all the ladies that I don't see how you can keep on top of all of this. Making dresses from scratch, altering them, new customers coming through the door every day. I do wish you would relax just a little." Marcus stood in front of her and put his arms around her waist.

"I think you might be right." Florence nodded.

The shop really had been a success, and almost from the beginning. She made fine dresses for middle-class women of Mrs Daventry's standard, often to their own specifications. But Florence had been determined that others should benefit too, and she continued to make a line of day-to-day dresses for the women of the working classes, women in service in the area of Wimbledon. Women like her grandmother, hard-working and of limited means.

She never expected that her shop would appeal to the finest of ladies, and she was glad about that. This was just what she wanted, and she couldn't have been happier.

"So, what do you say? Perhaps you should start advertising for a girl to come and help you." Marcus kissed the top of her head.

"I think I might need more than just one girl. I think I might need an experienced seamstress *and* a girl."

"I say!" Marcus said and looked truly surprised. "I didn't imagine that you'd ever loosen the reins, my dear. You're such a driven woman, are you sure there's room in here for another seamstress?" Marcus started to laugh, teasing her just the way he had always done.

"Tease all you like, but I have a very good reason for needing somebody to take my place for a while." She smiled slowly, staring into his bright blue eyes.

"Oh yes?" Marcus said, looking nonplussed.

"Do you really not take my meaning, Marcus? When you are the one who has his hands around my waist and doesn't realise how it's thickened?"

"Thickened?" he said and looked down at her. "I suppose you have a little..." he went on, and the realisation began to dawn. "Are you trying to tell me something, Mrs Daventry?"

"Yes, Mr Daventry," Florence said and laughed. "I'm trying to tell you that in a few short months, you're going to be a father."

"Oh, Florence!" he said, his eyes shining with emotion. "You clever, clever woman!" He lifted her off her feet and spun her around.

"Well, you did have a little something to do with it," Florence said and grinned.

"I do love you, my darling. I never thought, all those years ago as I watched you disappearing from Wimbledon with Queenie, that my life would ever be this happy. And never imagined that it would all work out in the end."

"Neither did I," Florence said and leaned against him. "I love you so much, Marcus."

"Oh, let's shut the shop early, shall we?" he said, his voice full of mischief and cajoling. "let's enjoy the rest of this day. We could go for a picnic on Wimbledon Common."

"A walk across the Common would be nice," Florence said and felt a great wave of contentment.

She would never forget her struggles, the pain of her life in Limehouse, not for as long as she lived. But she wouldn't let it define the rest of her life. She had been given a second chance at happiness, and she wasn't going to waste a minute of it.

As she slowly packed away her things ready to shut up the shop, Florence thought of her mother. She didn't have a memory of her at all, so she just imagined her as an older version of herself. She closed her eyes and pictured her face and wished with all her heart that Gladys Goodyear could have enjoyed just a little of the luck that had come to Florence.

Florence was twenty now, with the world at her feet. Twenty years old, just a little older than Gladys had been when she died. Even though she'd never known her, Florence would never forget her. She wasn't ashamed of her, she wasn't angry with her, she just missed her. Her only comforting thought was that there was somebody there in heaven keeping Queenie on the straight and narrow.

"What are you smiling at?" Marcus said, trying to break into her thoughts.

"I was just wondering if Queenie behaves herself in heaven," Florence said and laughed.

"I doubt it. She's probably hiding behind a cloud making gin and trying to sell it to the angels."

"Oh, Marcus!" Florence said and laughed. "I do believe you're right."

Thank you for Reading

I love sharing my Victorian Romances with you and as well as the ones I have published, I have several more waiting for my editor to approve.

I would love to invite you to join my exclusive Newsletter, you will be the first to find out when my books are available. It is FREE to join, and I will send you The Foundling's Despair as a thank you.

Read on for a preview of The Ratcatcher's Orphan

If you enjoyed this book please leave a review on Amazon or Goodreads, it will only take a moment and I would really appreciate it.

"Sooner or later, I will have to speak to Mrs Coleman about this dreadful girl. Really, Rupert, this must be absolutely the last time we employ an orphan," Mildred Collins said in a whisper so loud that Jane knew she was meant to hear it.

"Did we ever employ an orphan before this one?" Rupert Collins asked, not even bothering with the pretence of a whisper.

Jane Ashford, the orphan in question and the maid in Rupert and Mildred Collins' home for almost a year, made a very good pretence of not hearing a word her employers said. Instead, she continued to build a fire in the grate of the drawing room. Her hands were shaking a little as she did her best to make a neat and symmetrical pyramid out of the coals.

To Jane, this seemed like a ridiculous, pointless waste of time. Why on earth would anybody need an unlit fire to look so perfect when, at any moment, they might strike a match and have the whole thing devoured by flames? It was just another quirk of the upper classes as far as she could see, and it strangely made her glad that she was not among their number.

Of course, being an impoverished orphan who had been edged out of the orphanage at just twelve years of age was not a particularly comfortable set of circumstances either. Jane had been picked by Mildred Collins. The woman's harsh glare had surveyed the short line of terrified girls, all of a similar age, in order to pick one whom she thought at least looked clean and decent.

Jane hadn't forgotten that day in the year and a half which followed, nor was she ever likely to forget it. She had felt like one apple in a box of apples at the market, with the prospective buyer studying her and all the rest at close quarters. At the time, she imagined being picked up out of the box and turned over and over in Mildred Collins' hands while the woman checked for blemishes. It had been a horrible experience, a dehumanising experience, and Jane had decided there and then that she would never like the woman. As the year had passed by and Jane had reached the great age of thirteen and a half, nothing had changed; she still did not like Mildred Collins, only now she had more and more reasons in her experience for that feeling.

"My dear Rupert, would you look at the dreadful state of those coals!" Mildred said in a high-pitched whine. "Really, it will be a mercy when the whole thing is set alight, won't it?"

"I never saw anything so shoddy, my dear, never." Rupert spoke in a somewhat deeper version of Mildred's whine.

Still, Jane knelt before the fireplace and continued to work. She felt humiliated, that dreadful sensation of being watched making her suddenly clumsy. Her hands were shaking with anger as she wondered if that awful couple had anything more in common between them than their cruelty.

"Girl, girl?" Mildred began in a determined tone. "Rupert, what is her name again?" she said in that *out loud but under the breath* way, a style that was all her own.

"It is Jane, isn't it? Yes, it is Jane," Rupert added.

Jane bit down hard on her bottom lip. They both knew very well what her name was, but this was just one more tool in their upper-class box; it was designed to dehumanise her further still. What on earth did these dreadful people get out of such games? Slowly, Jane turned her head.

"Mrs Collins?" she said in a respectfully enquiring tone.

"No, no, do not look at me!" Mildred said, her eyes lighting up with glee. "There, now look what you have done!"

Jane turned back to look at the fireplace and saw that the tongs she was using had knocked the carefully placed coals all over the grate when she'd looked around at her mistress. It made her suddenly angry; it was all so unnecessary. Why couldn't they have just left her alone to get on with her work in peace? But no, they had to irritate her, anything to get their little bit of sport. Well, if that was where they found their joy, at least Jane could be glad that she was herself and not either one of them.

"I'm sorry, Mrs Collins," Jane said with practised deference as she began to rearrange the coals.

"At this rate, it will be dark before the fire is lit!" Mrs Collins said as if this was the greatest problem life had ever thrown at her; perhaps it was.

Jane could hear the enjoyment in the foul woman's voice, and it was all she could do to stoically re-stack the coals. This little piece of enjoyment was also contrived, so determined, and it made Jane angry. So angry that she closed her eyes and imagined striking Mrs Collins with the tongs.

She imagined Mrs Collins falling backwards in surprise, her peculiarly peach coloured hair, hair which must once have been a much more vibrant red, entirely disarranged as the mobcap she wore about the house when they didn't have visitors flew off. The image amused Jane a little and was just enough to break the anger. Jane needed this position and knew that her employers were capricious enough to dismiss her for the smallest of crimes. Losing her temper enough to even mildly complain about her treatment would certainly be enough to see her out on the streets. If only any other household in all of London had come to the orphanage that day looking to hire a maid. If only everything didn't feel so insecure, so uncertain.

Of course, Jane Ashford wouldn't be the only servant in London who felt as if her position was insecure, she knew that was the truth. However, nothing felt steady to Jane in that house as her employers see-sawed from cruelty to sense and then back again. But how would she escape them? If Jane were to leave and the Collins's didn't want her to go, Mrs Collins would simply not give her a reference. Jane knew that to have worked somewhere for more than a year and come out with no reference would make other households dubious of employing her. Oh, yes, Jane felt trapped all right.

Mr and Mrs Collins maintained their positions in the drawing room and watched Jane like hawks until the fire was finally set. Jane took a small cloth out of the pocket of her apron and wiped her hands clean before rising to her feet and getting ready to leave the room.

"Well, light it, girl," Rupert Collins said, shaking his head and tutting.

"Yes, sir." Jane reached for the box of matches on the mantle shelf. She struck one and lit the tag of paper she had left poking out between the coals. It was an easy lighting point. She gave it a moment or two before rising, seeing how well the fire took hold. She'd done a good job, whatever that miserable pair said.

"Will that be all?" Jane asked, her respectful tone so determined that it almost wasn't respectful at all. Still, she couldn't help but think that her privileged employers were too dull-witted to notice.

"Yes, that will be all," Mrs Collins said coolly.

Wasting no time, Jane hurriedly bobbed a small curtsy and headed for the door. As she reached it, she heard a clatter and a laugh and turned to see that Rupert Collins had used the poker in the fire to disarrange all the coals Jane had so painstakingly arranged. The laughter was Mildred's, clearly impressed by her husband's stupidity; what dreadful, privileged, pointless lives these people led.

"Would you just look at her, no better than she ought to be!" Mrs Coleman said with an angry click of her tongue.

Jane looked at her cautiously, then looked behind her. Mrs Coleman hardly ever spared her a word and certainly not in conversation. She gave her instructions, looked on disapprovingly, and that was that.

"Mrs Coleman?" Jane said in a quiet voice, certain that she must surely be mistaken; Mrs Coleman conversing with her? It was unheard of.

"Her, Miss Emma Talbot's maid! No better than she ought to be, I said!" She tipped her head in the direction of the window which looked out over the servants' yard beyond.

Jane followed her gaze to where a very fine-looking young woman was talking to Glyn Billington, the lad who delivered fruit and vegetables for the greengrocer.

Did Mrs Coleman have this right? The young woman certainly didn't look like any maid that Jane had seen before. Yes, she wore a dark dress, but it was nicely made, not the sort of thing Jane would ever expect to see a white canvas apron tied around. Her fair hair was in a bun, just as Jane's was, but there the similarity ended. She had little ringlets framing her face. Not so many as a fine lady might have, but it certainly seemed a little inappropriate for a servant. To top it all off, she was straight-backed and had a very obvious confidence about her.

"Are you sure she's Miss Talbot's maid, Mrs Coleman?" Jane asked, her curiosity giving her the courage to speak.

"Then you see what I do, Jane! No better than she ought to be!" Mrs Coleman said for the third time, and Jane wondered idly for a moment at the origins of such a ridiculous expression.

No better than she ought to be. It made no sense whatsoever, even though Jane knew exactly what it was meant to convey. It was a phrase she'd heard more than once as she'd grown up in the orphanage, a phrase that was designed to suggest that a woman suffered lax morals or was even a little promiscuous. Just as Jane was about to silently declare Mrs Coleman to be mistaken, she watched as Emma

Talbot's maid languidly reached out and took a shining red apple from the top of the box that Glyn Billington was carrying. The lad stood there simply looking at her, his mouth agape. The young woman was pretty enough, that was true, but not such a great beauty as to extract such an awe-laden response.

When the young woman bit into the apple, however, Jane felt her own mouth open. There was something provocative about it that she couldn't entirely explain, but there and then, she had a sense that Mrs Coleman might be right after all.

"Well, this won't get the house straight ready for the party, will it?" Mrs Coleman said with an uncustomary chuckle. "Right, Jane, I need you to check that all the guest bedrooms are fit and ready for tonight. I know they've already been done, but I don't want to chance it. I don't want one of the guests coming downstairs clutching a discarded polishing cloth like that dreadful vicar did last time!"

"Of course, Mrs Coleman," Jane said and darted away.

Jane crept about the upper corridors as silently as a cat, popping into one room after the other and carefully scouring each for any signs of forgotten cleaning materials. In no time at all, she was walking into the last of the rooms, having found nothing untoward thus far.

The final room was to be no different, although Jane lingered for a few minutes. This was to be the room that Emma Talbot stayed in, and Jane found herself thinking about the well turned out maid. The young woman was a lady's maid, of course, for that was the only type of maid who travelled with her mistress for a simple overnight stay. Lady's maids were always a little smarter, it was true, but that young woman might have passed for lower-middle-class, had it not been for that slight air about her. Had Miss Emma Talbot not noticed it? Or was it perhaps not obvious, something which the young woman had never let her mistress see?

Jane realised she was a little fascinated with the maid, wishing that she could work for an employer who would allow her better clothes, nicer hair. She tried to imagine Mildred Collins' reaction if Jane were to attend to her duties with her soft brown hair turned into ringlets at the front. She winced and shook her head; such a thing would not be tolerated; she knew that without a doubt.

Jane sighed and wandered over to the window, peering out over the rooftops and chimneys which pierced the pale blue sky. Not for the first time, Jane found herself wishing that she worked for anybody else in London. But perhaps not *anybody* else; perhaps somebody like Miss Emma Talbot.

The truth was, Jane, wished that there was another way to live, but people of her class, particularly orphans with no family to rely upon, had little choice in the matter. The whole system relied upon the existence of the poor, for who else would look after the seemingly useless rich? Jane didn't want to look after the useless rich, and she certainly didn't want to look after Mr and Mrs Collins. At night, she dreamed of a better life. Imagining that she had wealthy parents who had simply misplaced her, who had lost her through no fault of their own and had no idea that she had been discovered and placed in an orphanage.

She'd never known anything about her family, about the circumstances which surrounded her appearance at the orphanage as a baby. She'd asked, of course, but nobody had ever told her anything. The guardians at the orphanage were hardly any kinder than Mildred Collins, and Jane had always been told, as had each and every one of the other children, that she had likely been abandoned by a mother of loose morals. One who had enjoyed all the benefits of marriage without ever having spoken her vows. None of the spite stopped her wishing that she'd known her parents; her mother. It was like a gaping hole at the very core of her that would never, ever be filled.

"Well, this won't get the house straight for the party, will it?" she said, quietly parroting Mrs Coleman's words.

With a sigh, Jane turned from the window and wandered back across the room, taking a final look around to be certain that nothing had been left behind before she left the room and closed the door behind her

You can read The Ratcatcher's Orphan FREE with Kindle Unlimited

The Orphan in the Blue Satin Dress

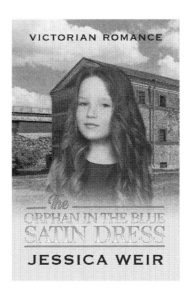

You can find all my books on Amazon, click the yellow follow button and Amazon will let you know when I have new releases and special offers.

Once again, thank you for being a fabulous reader and sharing this journey with me.

Printed in Great Britain
by Amazon